GORDO

GORDO

STORIES

JAIME CORTEZ

Black Cat
New York

FIRST EDITION

Published simultaneously in Canada
Printed in the United States of America

The following stories were previously published: "The Jesus Donut"
in *Kindergarde*, "El Gordo" on *Snap Judgment*, "The Nasty Book Wars"
(originally published as "The Nastybook Wars") in *Freeman's* and
Besame Mucho, "The Pardos" (originally published as "The Mercados")
in *2SexE*, and "Raymundo the Fag" in *Tea Party Magazine*.

This book is was set in 11.5-point Scala by Alpha Design & Composition
of Pittsfield, NH.

First Grove Atlantic paperback edition: August 2021

Library of Congress Cataloging-in-Publication data available for this title.

ISBN 978-0-8021-5808-6
eISBN 978-0-8021-5809-3

Black Cat
an imprint of Grove Atlantic
154 West 14th Street
New York, NY 10011

Distributed by Publishers Group West

groveatlantic.com

21 22 23 24   10 9 8 7 6 5 4 3 2 1

I dedicate this book to Felicitas and Felipe Cortez.
You loved me, you told stories, and you gave me an
extended master course in gallows humor.
I ask for nothing more.

Contents

GORDO

The Jesus Donut

S oon as the van turns off San Juan Highway onto our dirt
road, I can see the cloud of dust chasing it. Don't look
like nothing special at first. Just a white van changing into
a dusty brown van. When it gets closer, I see it says FLOUR
CHILD on the side in big curly letters. What does that mean?
The van stops close to me and the other kids, and the driver
opens the door and steps out. With his pink face, white shirt,
white hair, and little mustache, he looks like Mister Kentucky
Fried Chicken. My dog, Lobo, doesn't like strangers, and he
pulls on his chain and barks at the man.

Mister Kentucky opens up the two back doors of the
van. Of course, we're wondering what he's doing. Usually
the jefe, Joe Gyrich, is the only gringo that ever comes to
the Gyrich Farms Worker Camp, so it's not like we see real
Americanos here every day. Kentucky looks at us and smiles,
then he makes a little hook with his finger and calls us with
it. I point to myself, like I'm saying "me?"

"Yes you, my friend," he says. My cousin Cesar and me put down our sticks and stop our game of changai. My sister, Sylvie, and our cousins Olga and Tiny stop playing hopscotch and come over too. The five of us circle around Mister Kentucky, and he has a big ol' smile, like he's gonna tell us the greatest secret ever. "Hablan español?" he asks. I'm surprised to hear him talk in Spanish. It's like when I heard a parrot say "Lucy, I'm hoooome" at my tia's house. We didn't think he could do that. Then Cesar answers.

"Yeah, we can speak Spanish. English too." Cesar is so brave, talking to that big pink, white-haired gringo just like that. Maybe when I get to the sixth grade like him, I'll be all brave too.

"Muy bueno. That is very good," says Mister Kentucky real slow, like he thought we couldn't understand. Then he turns and opens up the two doors on the back of the van. Inside, it has four big silver metal drawers stacked up. He grabs the handle of the bottom drawer and pulls on it. It opens up, we look, and everyone is surprised.

"Waaaauw."

"Holy guacamole."

"Ooooh, so nice."

"No way, José."

The whole drawer is full up with donuts! Shiny, perfect donuts all in a row like little soldiers. The smell is really, really nice. We never had no van full of donuts arrive here at the Gyrich Farms Worker Camp before. Kentucky smiles at us, and we smile back at him. He shows us the next drawer.

Oh my God, Jesus. All chocolate donuts! Some of them have little rainbow sprinkles on them or even better: COCONUT. This chocolate drawer is so beautiful. Nobody says nothing. We stare. It's like a magic show. Kentucky is smiling so hard his eyes get tiny, and he opens the top drawer. One hundred percent cookies! I'm not lying, man. Huge cookies, bigger than your hand. Some oatmeal, some chocolate chip, and some yellow have-a-nice-day smiley face cookies too. It's a miracle. Someone bought a whole van filled up with donuts to the worker camp, here in the middle of the tomato fields in tiny San Juan Bautista. Nobody ever comes to the camp unless they work here or they're visiting the family.

"Please can I have one, please?" asks Tiny.

"No, stupid," says my sister, Sylvie. "They're not free. You gotta pay."

"How much I gotta pay?" asks Tiny.

"Not too much, little lady," says the man. "They're twelve cents each or two for twenty cents."

"Oh," says Tiny.

Nobody says nothing. I feel embarrassed. I don't have no twelve cents or even one cents. This nice man drives all the way out to the ranch, shows us the shiny donuts, and nobody has twelve cents to buy one. I think he is embarrassed too.

"Maybe you can ask your mama," he says.

"She's working," I say. I point to the tomato fields where my ma and the other mothers are working. Mister Kentucky thinks and then he says, "All righty, well, maybe next time you can save your pennies and buy a donut, my friend." He closes the cookie drawer, then the beautiful chocolate drawer, and then Olga says, "Wait, please. Can I please have two donuts, please?"

"Of course you can, little lady," says Kentucky. "What kind of donuts would you like?" Everyone's staring at Olga, cuz—where did she get money? The man gets a pink-and-white bag and a little piece of paper.

"Please, I want a chocolate donut with rainbow sprinkles, please," she says. The man gets one and puts it in the bag. Then she points to the shiny glazed donuts on the bottom drawer. He pops one of those in the bag too.

"Twenty cents," he says.

Everybody stops breathing. What's she gonna do? She don't got no money. She gonna take the bag and run? That would be stupid, cuz he could chase her in the van. Besides, if she did that, Grandma would hit her so hard, she'd see the Devil through a hole. I don't know what that means, but Grandma always says that, and it sounds pretty serious.

Olga bends down and unties one of her tennies. She takes it off her foot and there, in the bottom of the stinky shoe, is a perfect, shiny quarter! She picks it up, wipes it on her dress, and gives it to him. Mister Kentucky takes the quarter and puts it into the change machine on his belt. He pops out a nickel and gives it to her. It's like a present.

"Thank you, darling," he says.

"Thank you, mister," she says.

"Anyone else?" he asks. No one says yes. No one says no. So he smiles and closes up the drawers, shuts the back doors, and gets into the van. He drives away slowly, waves at us one time, and then goes faster down the road. We stand around Olga.

"Where'd you get that money?" asks Cesar.

"My papi gave me two quarters for my domingo cuz I helped out in the house."

"They PAY YOU to help in the house?" asks Sylvie. She's really surprised that Olga got paid. I can't believe it either.

"Liar!" says Sylvie. "Nobody gets paid to help around the house."

"Believe it or don't. I got paid," says Olga. She looks really happy.

"Hey, Olga," says Tiny. "What you gonna do with that extra donut?"

"It's not an *extra* donut, bonehead!" says Cesar. "You know what she's gonna do? She's gonna scarf those donuts up. Both of them." His voice sounds like something that got dropped and then broke.

"I'm just asking, that's all," says Tiny. I think she wants to cry. I don't blame her.

"You guys want some donut?" says Olga.

"Reeeeeally?" I ask.

"Yeah," she says. She's gonna share the fancy donuts! I can hardly believe it.

"Heck yeah, I want some!" says Cesar.

"You can have some," she says. "But you have to do what I say, and you can't taste the chocolate one."

"Well what do we have to do?" asks Sylvie.

"First, you cochinos have to wash your dirty hands and your faces and fix your hair, like on Sunday."

"What for?" asks Sylvie.

"I don't have to tell you what for. If you want donut, you have to do it," Olga says. So we go into the big shower room where everybody goes to clean up after work. There are two big sinks and three showers. We use the big brown brick of Lirio soap to wash our faces. I wet my hair and push the wild curls down with my hands. I dry my hands on my pants like Cesar, and we all walk back out.

"Now you have to get in a line on your knees," says Olga.

"This is STOOPID!" shouts Cesar.

"If you don't like it, go away, Cesar. But if you want donut, do what I say!" Dang. Olga's brave like Cesar. Cesar thinks for a moment, and he gets on his knees. One by one, we all do the same and get in line. Olga goes to the first person. It's Sylvie. She cuts off a little piece of donut between two fingers, holds it next to Sylvie's mouth, and says, "Body of Christ."

Sylvie says, "Amen."

"STOP!" says Cesar. "Everybody knows girls can't be no priests, and you can't pretend to do Holy Communion, man. That's blasphemy!" Olga don't care. She puts the little piece of donut on Sylvie's tongue. Sylvie closes her mouth and she kneels there, really quiet, with a little smile on her face. Cesar points his finger at Olga's face and shouts, "I'm

6

not gonna do blasphemy for no donut, pendeja!" Cesar looks at me and says, "C'mon, Gordo. Let's get outta here." He walks away and in a few steps he looks back and sees me on my knees.

"Are you coming with me, Gordo?" he asks me.

"I will. As soon as I get some donut." Cesar looks at me, and I think I'm in trouble.

"You know what, man?" says Cesar. "If you stay here, you can't hang around with me no more."

Oh man. This is serious. I want to follow him around 50 percent, but I want donut like 90 percent, so I stay. Cesar nods his head and walks away, kicking up dirt at us, like a cat burying poop.

Olga goes down the line and gives everyone some Jesus donut. I am the second to the last, and I watch while she gives everybody Communion, they go *mmm*, and the donut gets smaller and smaller. The little rocks I'm kneeling on hurt my knees. I keep thinking that I should have put myself first in line, then I wouldn't have to be kneeling in the dirt, afraid the donut will finish before it gets to me. But lucky for me, when she finally gets to me, there's a lot of donut left. She cuts off a little piece, looks at me, and says, "Body of Christ."

"Amen," I say, and I open my mouth. She puts the piece of donut on my tongue. I close my mouth. I close my eyes. Mmm.

This is the way Jesus should taste.

* * *

Yeah, it should be like this in church. When you have the Body of Christ on your tongue, it should taste like a sweet donut cloud that gets tinier and tinier in your mouth, and then it disappears, and you know he's good.

The last piece of donut is almost half the donut. Way bigger than what we got. Olga pushes the whole thing into her mouth and eats it all herself. She chews and chews like a little cow, then she finishes. She wipes her hands on her dress, then opens them up like two wings and says, "You may go in peace, this mass is over."

She walks away, swinging her pink-and-white bag. We get up and clean our knees. Olga gets to her house and pulls open the screen door with the rips so big a billy goat could walk through, then she goes inside. Soon as she disappears, everyone starts talking at the same time about Olga and the Jesus donut.

"That was good."

"That was loco."

"Yeah, she's crazy."

"She's nice. She gave me donut, so I don't care what she did."

"That really was blasphemy. People shouldn't do blasphemy. It's bad."

"We should have beat her up, then took the donut. It's only right."

"What a little pig. She ate half of it herself."

"She made us get in the dirt and wash our faces for one little tiny crumb."

"Nobody forced you, so stop complaining. Besides, it was dee-licious!"

Everybody thinks something different, but the more I think about it, the more I hate Olga and her donut. The way she pretended she was a priest. Cesar was right. Girls can't be priests anyways, so no way can she do a Communion. Just then, Olga comes back out of her house like she forgot something. When she gets close enough to hear, we stop talking about her.

"Church will be tomorrow at twelve in the afternoon in my kitchen," says Olga.

"You're gonna let us have the chocolate donut?" asks Tiny.

"Yup. Body of Christ at twelve o'clock," she says.

"Right on, sister!" says Sylvie. Olga has a big smile on her face, like she's a big deal. I guess she is. She goes back into her house and right before she closes the door, she says, "See you at twelve o'clock. Don't be late. Later, alligator."

That night when I go to sleep, I don't really go to sleep. I go to worry. I keep thinking about that chocolate donut. If the glazed donut tasted like Jesus, what does the chocolate donut taste like? If the chocolate donut is even better, but it's smaller than the glazed donut, it's not fair that we can only have a tiny taste, and then we have to watch her eating with so much donut in her trap she can't even close it. Maybe I should have walked away from the blasphemy like Cesar did. Now I'm suffering, so maybe I'm getting punished for pretending the donut was the Body of the Lord God Jesus Christ. I don't know. I only know I want to have some more donut, no matter what.

The next morning, me and Sylvie get up, make our bunks, and have breakfast with Ma and Pa. After we eat, I help my pa wash the car, vacuum the car, then wax the car. I hate waxing. He gets so mad. "Do it harder! Do it faster! Don't let the wax dry too much, muchacho. What's the matter with you?!" Jesus. You want it so perfect, you do it! That's what I want to say to my pa, but I don't want to get smacked on the head, so I keep on waxing. When I grow up and get my own car, I'm never gonna wax no matter what. At 11:38, we finish. Pa says go wash up for lunch. I say okay, but instead I go and wait in front of Olga's house for church. Sylvie and Tiny arrive. Their faces are washed and their hair is all shiny. Then Olga comes out.

"You can enter the house of the Lord now, brothers and sisters," she says. We open the door and go into the kitchen.

"Please kneel," Olga says. We get on our knees like before.

"For what we are about to receive," she says.

"Let us be truly thankful," we say. She goes to the cupboard where she hid the donut. She moves a little sack of flour and a can of Café Combate. She pulls out a little plate with the donut. She looks down at it. "Oh no!" she says real soft. Then she shouts, "OH NO!"

The donut is covered with black ants! Millions of them. There's so many that the donut looks like it's wearing a black sweater. We all say, "Ewwwww!" and "Gross, man!" And the ants crawl off the plate and up her hand. Olga tries to squish them, but there are too many. She takes the donut to the sink and hits it against the side to knock the ants off, but they keep crawling up her hand. Then we really get laughing and making all kinds of fun of her.

"Ha ha! You shoulda shared the donut when you had a chance, bonehead!"

"Yeah, Olga, you can take your ant-flavored donut and stick it up your butt!"

"We told you it was blasphemy. Now look what happened!"

She turns on the water and puts the donut under it and tries to clean it, but instead it breaks into pieces with wet, drowned ants all over it like sprinkles!

"You can't wash a donut, retard!" I say, and everybody's laughing. Olga starts to cry. The more she cries, the more we laugh, till finally she shouts, "Get out!" And she grabs a broom and swings it like a mom and smacks me in the shoulder, but I don't care, cuz I'm laughing so good. We run outta the house like rabbits, and we can't stop laughing because Olga's mass is finished, and now we can laugh to the sky, because laughing about the broken, wet donut with the ant sweater is even better than eating it!

El Gordo

It's Sunday morning. We went to morning Mass at the mission in San Juan Bautista, like always. My ma and Sylvie are visiting my nana next door, like always. Pa is at the Big Red Barn Flea Market, like always. I'm home alone in my bunk, lying on my stomach, eating Fritos, and reading, like always. *Encyclopedia Brown Saves the Day* is so cool. I would definitely be friends with Encyclopedia Brown if I went to his school. I hear the station wagon park in the spot right next to my window. Pa is home from the flea market. I hear him open the front door, call my name, and stomp across the kitchen right into me and Sylvie's little bedroom. Right away, I can smell beer, but not too much.

"Surprise!" he says. He's a little drunk, but he's not mad, so even though my ma's not home, I think I'll be okay. Maybe. He puts a big box down on the floor right next to my bed. It's wrapped up with rope tied in a messed-up bow on top. My nickname, "Gordo," is written on it in my pa's big, ugly letters.

"What's that?" I ask.

"A present," says Pa. It's not my birthday and it's not Christmas. I'm surprised to get a present.

"Really, Pa? For me?" I ask.

"Correcto. It's yours, Gordo."

"Why?"

"Just because," says Pa. Oh my God. My first just-because present! I shake the box. It's heavy and it sounds like there's all kinds of things in there.

"Can I open it?" I ask. Pa smiles and nods his head. I pull and pull on the rope, and even though it's not thick, it's really strong and I can't get it off the box. Pa starts laughing, takes out his pocketknife, and pulls out the blade.

"Here. Use this, Gordo," says Pa. "Pero cuidado, don't cut yourself." I get the knife and hold it in my hand. The handle is made of chrome and red wood. It feels warm and heavy. It's super beautiful, and I've always wanted to hold it. Pa's knife is really sharp, and in one swipe, I cut the rope off the box and open the top.

Oooooh. All kinds of things are in the box. It's a present full of more presents! I see bags, boxes, and stuff wrapped in plastic. I pull out the first thing. It's a black, leather . . . thing. It looks like a flat pear.

"All right!" I say.

"You like it?" asks my pa.

"I think so. What is it?"

"It's a speed bag. Like a punching bag, hijo," says Pa. "We gotta put some air in it, hang it up, and then you can

13

start punching with theeeeese," he says. He rips open a blue paper bag and pulls out two puffy red gloves that make me think of clown shoes. I laugh at them.

"What's so funny?" asks Pa.

"Nothing. They look kind of funny. Puffy."

"They're not funny. They're boxing gloves. You can use them to hit the punching bag and maybe hit somebody in the ring one day." He punches the air and says, "Poom!"

"Oh," I say.

So far, this is a bad present.

"Where'd you get all this boxing stuff?" I ask Pa.

"At the pulga, of course. The árabes, they having new things for the boys today. Boxing and lucha libre wrestling things. People were buying it like pan caliente. Look in the box, hijo, there's more," he says. Inside the big box, there is a smaller box. I open it up. Shiny white boxer boots with silver stripes and shoelaces and little dangly pom-poms on the side!

"Thank you," I say. "These are soooo pretty!" Pa gets real quiet. He opens his mouth like he's gonna say something, but he don't say nothing. He shakes his head like something bad just happened. I'm holding my boots like little twin babies, telling him they're so pretty, and then he breathes like he's really tired and says, "Keep going, hijo."

I reach into the box, grab a folded-up bag, and open it up. Yeeeessss! A lucha libre mask of my favorite wrestler, El Santo! The mask covers your whole head and face in sparkly silver. Even the mouth hole and eyeholes are sparkly.

"It's all for you, hijo! Keep going," he says. There is a bag in the box, and I open it up.

"A jump rope! Wow, Pa! This is the best thing!" I feel like maybe I'm going to cry. I look up at Pa. I almost can't say it, but finally I say, "Gracias, Papi. I've been wanting my own jump rope forever. Sylvie never wants to loan me hers. But now, anytime I want to, I can play jump rope."

"It's not for playing," says Pa. "It's for ejercicio. Understand? You start training and training, so your heart and your legs can get fuerte, and you can burn off the fat, get strong to do boxing. Lucha libre. Entiendes?"

"I understand, Pa."

"Hijo, you know how Muhammad Ali is the black Superman?"

"Yeah, he's the best."

"Well, Gordo, you can be the brown Superman. 'Float like a butterfly, sting like a bee'! Un gran campeón!"

"Okay."

"All you need to do is train hard. You want to put on your Santo mask?"

"Yes, Pa!"

I grab it and try to put it on, but I can't. Pa takes it from me and unties the laces on the back of the mask and opens it up. Then he puts it on my head and pulls it down hard. I can feel him tying the laces in the back. When he finishes, it's really tight, and it's pulling my hair, and my ear is kind of bent, and it hurts, but I don't care. I love it.

"Turn around, Gordo," says Pa. "Look at yourself." I walk over to the mirror. Wow. I'm pretty sure I look cool. My pa stands behind me. I hold up my arms and make a muscle, and he reaches down and tries to pull off my shirt. I don't want to take off my shirt in front of him or nobody, and I grab it and yank it back down.

"Gordo," he says. "Take it off."

"I don't want—"

"Take it off. Now."

With my shirt off, I feel naked, and I don't like it. He tells me to look in the mirror again, so I do. I look even more like El Santo now! He is smiling. I feel like El Santo. This is boss.

"You wanna try on your boots?" he asks.

"Yes." I sit down on my bed, and Pa takes off my shoes, opens up the laces of the boots, and puts them on my feet. Then he tightens them up and ties them. I stand up. I bounce up and down, and they don't weigh nothing. I feel like an astronaut, like I can jump up to the top of the house like Lee Majors, the Bionic Man. And they're so pretty. I've never had such a beautiful thing before. I jump up and down some more because it feels so good, and my pa grabs me and hugs me and lifts me up like I was a little boy or something.

"Let's go outside so I can teach you jumping the rope," says Pa.

"I already know how to jump rope, Pa," I say. "When I play with Sylvie and the girls, I can beat them sometimes." I grab my rope and follow him. I don't ever go outside with my shirt off, even at the beach. It's embarrassing to be fat. I don't like the way people look at me. But today, I don't care. I'm El Santo, and I'm the best. I pick a spot in front of the house, and I begin jumping rope.

My pa looks pretty excited when he sees me jump. My dog, Lobo, comes running to see what's going on.

"Caramba, Gordo! You got good reflexes, mijo, good feet!" he says. I never seen my father so happy before. And I start to jump faster and faster, and when the rope hits the ground, little rocks and dust pop right up. My papi is watching me, and he's laughing and so excited. He even jumps up and down a few times. Lobo is excited too. His tail is wagging and he starts barking. I start to sing my favorite jump rope song that I learned from Sylvie.

I'm a little princess
Dressed in blue.
Here are the things
I like to do:
Salute to the captain,
Bow to the queen,
Turn my back
On the submarine.
I can do the tap dance,
I can do the splits—

"DON'T!" he yells. I stop.
"Don't what?" I ask.

"Don't sing that song." I'm breathing hard from the jumping, but I'm also thinking hard. I look at his face. If the next thing I say is the wrong thing, I'm gonna get hit.

"Should I sing a different song?" I ask.

"No, hijo. No singing. All you do is jump and count, jump and count, okay? Every day you training, you trying to jump a little more."

"Okay," I say. "I'll count." I jump faster and count like he told me to. Now I'm starting to get nervous, and I start to miss. Every time I miss, I start again and try harder and harder. My face feels hot in the Santo mask, and I want to take it off, but I don't stop jumping. My legs are burning, and I am in a cloud of dust, but Pa looks happier now, and I think he's not gonna hit me, and he's not gonna shout. That's not bad.

"Caramba," he says. "That's good. You're big, but you're fast, hijo. Practice, practice. If you jump fifty times today, jump sixty tomorrow, then one hundred, then one day one thousand. I think you can be a good boxer. You want to box?"

"I don't know. Maybe."

"Try. You can do it."

"Okay, I'll try."

"I gotta take a shower now, hijo. You keep training, okay?"

"Yes."

I start jumping rope and counting. It's not as fun as singing, but it's okay. Lobo lies down in the dirt. I think he's bored with the counting, like me. After Pa walks away, I start singing instead. I whisper at first. I can't tell you the name of the song. It's only for me.

It's getting hotter and hotter in the mask. I stop jumping, and I'm starting to untie the laces in the back. It's hard because they're so tight. I'm getting frustrated, and I want to get a knife and cut it off. I wish someone could help me. Then I hear somebody behind me say, "Hey, you!"

I stop untying the mask and look behind me. It's Miguelito from across the camp. He has a Santo mask too and kneepads and a blue cape! He is not wearing no shirt and you can see all his bones in his chest. But the cape is really shiny and pretty, and he looks good, standing there with his bony legs open like a superhero's.

"You think you're the best," says Miguelito. "But you're not, Gordo."

"I didn't say I was the best," I tell him.

"But you think you're the best. Training with your rope. You think you're the boss. But you're not."

"I didn't say I was the best."

"But you're wearing the Santo mask, *ese*," says Miguelito. "And Santo is the best, so you think you're the best."

"You're wearing the same mask, pendejo," I tell Miguelito. "Where did you get your mask?"

"My dad got it for me at the flea today," he says.

"My pa did too. Did he get you boots and a jump rope and a punching bag?" I ask.

"No. I got the mask, cape, kneepads, so I'm ready to fight. Man, we have to have a battle. You know that old mattress someone threw out behind the tractor barn?" asks Miguelito.

"Yeah, the one we jump on?"

"Yup. We can have a championship fight on that mattress. I challenge you. You're El Gordo."

"I'm not El Gordo," I tell Miguelito. "I'm El Santo. Can't you see my mask?"

"No you're not," says Miguelito. "We both got the same mask, but we can't both be El Santo. If we have a championship fight of the world on the mattress, we can see who gets to be El Santo of . . . the Gyrich Farms Worker Camp. If you lose, you're El Gordo forever."

"Okay, but if I'm El Gordo then you're El Flaco, cuz you're so skinny."

"Okay, I'll be El Flaco. I don't care what you call me, man, because I'm calling you out right now. I'm going to beat you," says Miguelito. "Then I'll rip off your mask so everyone will see who you really are: big, fat, greasy Gordo." Now I'm mad.

"I'm going to break your nose and your femur." I tell him.

"What the fuck is a femur?" says Miguelito.

"It's your leg bone, idiot," I tell him. "Don't you know nothing? I'm gonna tear off your femur and hit you with it like a caveman." Miguelito is getting mad too, and he starts to shout.

"You ain't no big deal, man, just because you're always lying on your butt reading books. Nobody thinks you're a big deal with your books."

We walk out together to the mattress. My dog, Lobo, follows us. The mattress is leaning on the back wall of the tractor barn. We drag it to a place where the ground is flat. Then we begin jumping around on the mattress. The mattress is big, so we have room to move around. My boots feel great. I feel great.

"You ready, Flaco?" I ask him.

"I'm ready for round one," he says. "Ding ding ding!" He begins making animal noises at me, like a bear or something. Lobo looks up at our faces, and he begins growling. Miguelito says, "WOOF!" at Lobo, real loud. Lobo jumps back a little bit like he's scared, then he starts barking, and he starts going around the mattress in circles, barking at us. Me and Miguelito walk around each other and then he backs up into a corner and points to the middle of the mattress.

"You see that big stain in the middle of the mattress?" he says to me. "Someone peed there, probably some drunk old hobo, and when I beat you, I'm gonna mash your face in his pee."

"You wish," I say. "I'm going to make you lick it up like a dog!"

He puts his hands out in front of him. He bends his fingers so they look like claws. He charges at me and pushes his head into my stomach. I go "oof!" and then I fall back on the mattress. He jumps on me and grabs me by the neck and starts strangling me. Dang. Miguelito is fast! I roll and he rolls with me and now I'm on top! I grab him by the hands and start pushing them down till I have him crucified on the mattress. His blue cape is all twisted up around his neck, but he never stops fighting. Miguelito is super strong for a skinny little dude. He jams his knee against my stomach, then his feet, and he pushes me back. I fall back and suddenly he's on top of me and trying to crucify me. Lobo is barking and barking, and I roll myself over and start to get up, and he jumps on my back and wraps his arms around my neck like a monkey. I fall on my knees and try to get his arms off of me, but I can't. He's really got me now. I stand up, and he's still holding on with his arms and knees. Then I fall backward and land on top of him, and he rips a big fart.

Everything stops.

I scream. He screams. And we both start laughing. While he's still laughing, I flip around and grab him by the neck like I'm going to strangle him, and I say, "You're not El Flaco, you're the Stinkbug! Lobo runs onto the mattress and starts licking Miguelito's mask.

"NO! Stop it, Lobo. Go away. Bad boy!" Lobo stops licking his face and backs off. Miguelito gets up. His mask is crooked now, and his eyeholes are all wrong. He fixes his mask.

"Hey," says Miguelito. "You know how to do the airplane?"

"Yeah, I know," I say.

"Let's do the airplane then!"

"I grab him by one arm and one leg, and I lift him off the ground and begin to spin in circles. He is shouting: "You'll never beat me!" I spin him around faster and faster, and he's laughing and screaming, and Lobo is going crazy, barking and barking. I feel strong, like a big giant superhero, like we're both flying! Then it's too fast and my hands aren't strong enough, and I lose my grip. Miguelito goes flying past the mattress and he skids into the dirt on his face and chest. Poor Miguelito says, "UGH!" And then worst of all, Lobo runs up behind him and bites him on the shoulder. Miguelito screams. I jump in and grab Lobo by the neck and try to pull him off, but it's hard because Lobo is big and angry and when he looks at me, it's like he doesn't know me anymore. When I get Lobo off of Miguelito, Lobo's mouth is bleeding. Oh no. Maybe that's Miguelito's blood. Maybe Lobo bit himself on the tongue. I don't know. This is bad. "Bad boy!" I say to Lobo, and slap him on the head. He escapes out of my hands and runs away. I go to Miguelito. His mask is all crooked, but I can see part of his mouth. It is wide open. He is crying.

"Lobo bit me. Your fucking dog bit me. Did you see all that blood on Lobo's mouth?"

"I think maybe the blood was Lobo's blood. He bit his own tongue."

I stand on the mattress, breathing hard. Miguelito is still lying down and crying, but he's hardly making any sounds. His brand-new mask has blood around the mouth and nose holes, and he has a big raspberry on his chest from skidding in the dirt and two little bloody marks that look like vampire bites on his shoulder, where Lobo bit him.

Miguelito fixes his mask. I can see his eyes are red.

"Why'd you drop me, Gordo?"

"I'm sorry, man," I say. My voice is tiny. "It was an accident. I couldn't hold on. I'm sorry."

"You shouldn't of dropped me. I think I broke my shoulder."

"You can't break your shoulder. Shoulders don't break."

"I'm bleeding."

"I tried to hold on to you," I say. "But I couldn't."

"I'm going to tell my dad on you, Gordo."

"Don't Miguelito. I'll fix you up, okay? Don't tell him, man. Your dad is the meanest of all the dads. If you tell him what happened, he'll probably hit you instead of me." Miguelito thinks for a moment, and we're both quiet, then someone shouts at us.

"Hey! What the hell happened?" It's my pa. He's walking to us. His hair is still wet from the shower. When he gets close, I can see Pa has a little bloody tissue on his chin from shaving.

"Get up, Miguelito," says my pa. Miguelito stands up. Pa takes the laces off Miguelito's mask and pulls it off. Pa holds Miguelito's face and looks at it, like a doctor. Miguelito has a little blood under his nose and his lip has a cut. Pa looks at me and asks, "What happened?" I'm about to tell him what happened, but Miguelito goes first.

"I told Gordo we had to have a fight to see who is the champion of Gyrich Farms. We started fighting, then we were doing the airplane, and Gordo let go of me and I crashed into the dirt and broke my shoulder and cut my face. And stupid Lobo bit me."

"So you asked for a fight, Flaco?" asks my pa.

"Gordo dropped me and—"

"Did you ask for a fight?"

"I guess so," says Miguelito.

"Yes he did," I say. "I wasn't doing nothing and Miguelito called me out and I had to fight him, and we had an accident."

"Miguelito," says my pa. "Gordo's about twenty pounds more heavier than you. He's taller too. If a little guy like you tells a big guy he wants to fight, what do you think happens?"

Miguelito is quiet, then he says, "I don't know."

"Usually, you get beat up," says Pa.

"But my shoulder's broken," he says.

"Let me see your shoulder," says Pa. "Can you lift your arm?" Miguelito raises his arm. Dad gets Miguelito by the elbow and moves the arm up and down, bends it back, then moves it in circles.

"Don't worry, Flaco," my pa says. "Only scratches, nothing broken. Tu estas perfectamente bien. Do you want me to clean your cuts and put mercurio on it?" asks Pa.

"No," says Miguelito. "Mercurio hurts, and it looks like blood."

"Then go home to your mami, stop crying, and start training so you can win the next fight."

"I didn't lose the fight," says Miguelito. "It only looks like I lost. He dropped me."

"Look at your face with blood. Look at Gordo's face. Who won?"

"Your dog bit me," says Miguelito. Dad looks at the bite marks.

"Pfft. No es nada. Lobo was just playing. Baby bites. Go home, wash it, and get some mercurio on it, like I told you."

25

Miguelito looks at my pa like he wants to say something back, but he don't say nothin'. Miguelito gets up and fixes his cape and then walks past me. As he passes, Miguelito mad dogs me. I say I'm sorry one more time. Miguelito looks at me and he talks, but he doesn't make a sound. I can see his mouth moving slowly, and he is saying: "Fuck you." I look down at my pretty silver boots.

"Gordo," says my pa.

"What?" I ask.

"You won."

Pa squeezes my shoulder and smiles at me. Then he walks away. I sit down on the mattress. I reach back and open up the laces on the back of my mask. I pull it off. Aah. My hair is wet. My face is hot. The air feels good, but I don't feel good. Lobo walks back to me and lays down next to me on the mattress. He still has a little blood on his mouth.

"Hey, Lobo," I say. He looks at me. He looks kind of sad.

"I won," I tell him. "I won."

Chorizo

The dogs are melting. Lobo is lying on the porch with his pink tongue hanging out. Chiquita is hiding under the car with her ears down. Everybody is hiding from the sun except for me. I'm riding my bicycle so I can feel some wind when I pedal. It's not working too good. Past the tomato fields, I can see this family walking along San Juan Highway. Right away I know they ain't doing so good. We're not rich or nothing, but they look super poor, even from far away. They're walking, so obviously they don't have no car or even a bike. I see two adults and two kids. The mom and dad have big Santa Claus sacks on their backs. The two kids have smaller sacks. They turn off of the highway and start walking up the dirt road to the Gyrich Farms Worker Camp.

"Somebody's coming!" I tell my nana. "Who are they?" Nana looks out the kitchen window. "Only God knows, mijo."

"Are they in our family?" I ask.

"I don't think so, Gordo."

"Do you think they're lost?"

"Maybe. We'll see," she says.

They get closer and I can see them clearly. They're indios. They're darker than Hershey Bar Pancho, and he's the blackest in the family. Their faces are sweaty. The little girl wears huaraches, and her feet are dirty from the road. They get to my nana's house and stand in a row. I say hi. They look embarrassed.

"Hola," I say.

Nana comes out. The mom and dad smile at her.

"Buenos dias, señora," the father says. His voice sounds like a joke voice. Like he's trying to sound like a girl. I look at him more carefully. His boots are tiny, smaller than mine. I never seen such a tiny man. He holds out his tiny brown hand and Nana cleans the soap off her hands, and they shake.

They introduce themselves. The father's name is Xaman. The mother is Yuritzi. I never heard names like those before. Those are *Star Trek* alien names.

"Señora," says the father. "We're sorry to bother you, but we have a great favor to ask."

"Tell me."

"If you could, señora. Would you make us a gift of a glass of water?" I never heard of nobody giving a gift of water. That would suck, to get a gift that was just a glass of water.

"Yes. Of course. Please sit here on the porch, out of the sun."

"Gracias. The children, they're very thirsty."

"It's so hot today. Poor kids look tired," says Nana. She pats the girl's dusty head. "I'll get a nice pitcher of cold water."

Nana goes into the kitchen. The family sits down in the shade of the porch. Lobo is too hot to bark. The two kids sit down on their sacks. The little girl stares at my bike like she'd never seen a bike before. The boy could be my grade or maybe just a third grader. You can't really say, because even though his head is really big, his body is tiny. His hair shoots up like Woody Woodpecker's. I can hear Nana cracking the ice and then she comes out with a pitcher of water and four stacked glasses. She gives everyone a full glass, and they drink it to the bottom. Nana fills them up again and they finish it all real fast.

"Nana, they're super thirsty," I say. "Maybe we should let 'em drink from the hose."

"Niño. Be quiet." She says to me and says to the father: "I'm sorry, señor. He talks too much. Please excuse him."

"No, he's right," says Xaman. "We could probably drink a gallon each." Yuritzi smiles and nods her head.

"We've been walking since the little store in town," she says. She also has the voice of a little kid.

"Ave Maria," says Nana. "You've been walking from Sanchez Superette? The red store with the wooden bear in the front?"

"Yes. We walked from there. We're looking for work. Do you have work, señora? We'll do anything."

"This isn't our rancho. We're only workers here, señor."

"Do you think your jefe would hire us? We'll do anything."

"You might be in luck. It's August. The tomato harvest started this week. Yesterday the migra came with two vans and grabbed a bunch of workers off the tomato harvester to send them back to Mexico, so the jefe might need extra hands." The little man leans forward and grabs Nana's hand.

"Do you think maybe you could possibly help us meet your jefe to ask for work?"

"Yes," says Nana. "It's heavy work, though, especially on the tomato harvester. They only hire women. Their hands are smaller and faster." Nana looks at the mom. "Señora, I've worked the harvester many times," warns Nana. "With the heat and the dust and the noise, lots of women faint."

"No hay problema," says the father, slapping Yuritza's shoulder. "This one, she's like a mule. Strong." That's pretty funny. The mom smiles at her feet. When the little girl smiles, I can see all of her front teeth are gone except for the two pointy ones on the side. Every kid in the Gyrich Farms Worker Camp has to have a nickname. I decide hers will be Vampi.

"Our jefe usually passes by in the mornings to load up the water truck at the pump right over there. We can ask him then."

"Yes, por favor, let's do that. We have to thank the Virgin for putting you in our path, señora, to help us find work. Gracias."

"Let's hope we can get you some work," says Nana.

"It shames me to ask for another favor."

"Go on, señor."

"That building over there. Can we sleep there?"

"That's for the chickens, señor. I couldn't let you sleep there. It's too dirty. There's fleas. Lice."

"How about over there," he asks, pointing to the carport.

"In the carport?" asks Nana.

"We promise we'll take good care of it."

"There's shade, but there are no walls," says Nana.

"That's all we need, señora. We're very tired. We'll only stay a couple of days, until we find work."

"I'm sorry we don't have room in the house, but it's tomato season, and we have cousins staying and the house is really full. We're like sardines, but if you want to sleep in the carport you can."

"Thank you, señora. May God reward you for this."

After resting in the shade and drinking some more water, the family begins taking their stuff out. First, they take out a big blue plastic sheet and lay it out on the dirt. Then they put a big dirt clod on each corner of the sheet. They're going to sleep on that? They unfold another plastic sheet and with a yellow rope they make a little tent, like if they're camping. Vampi's mom gets the hose, turns it on, and—I can't believe it—Vampi and her brother get naked, completely naked, and she hoses them and soaps and then washes their hair. Nana stomps out of the house, walks over to me, and points for me to go inside, so I do. She follows after me.

"Gordo," she says. "Stop staring at that family."

"They're taking a bath outside," I say.

"Let them," she says. "They're trying to get clean. There's nothing wrong with that. I'd be happy if you'd take a bath inside or outside or anywhere." Grandma steps back outside and talks to the mom. I stand near the window and pretend not to watch them all.

"Yuritzi," says Nana. "Do you and your husband want to use the shower room over there by the willow tree?"

"Yes, gracias."

"We don't have indoor toilets here at the camp," says Nana. "The outhouses are over there for you all to use. There's paper there already. There is a flashlight in there if you need to use it at night. Also, we don't have a telephone here. I'm sorry." The lady and her husband begin to giggle. "Ai, señora," she says. "It doesn't matter if you don't have a telephone. In our pueblo, no one in the family has a telephone. There's nobody to call!" Nana laughs with them.

"Do you want to use the kitchen? I have a stove and sink and refrigerator if you want to use them."

"No. That's fine."

"Please don't be shy about asking for anything."

"Gracias," says Yuritzi. Nana goes back inside and I follow her. A few minutes later, we hear my grandpa pulling up in his pickup truck. He is home from work. He drives to his usual parking spot in the carport but stops when he sees the family. Grandpa gets out of the pickup. He don't say hi or nothing to the family. He walks straight into the house.

"Vieja, who are those people?" he asks Nana.

"They just arrived from the other side. They don't have any place to sleep." He don't say nothing. She don't say nothing.

"Gordo, go outside," says Grandpa.

"But Grandpa," I say, "Nana just told me to stay inside."

"And I'm telling you to go outside. And don't bother those people."

I step out and ride my bicycle around the house like a merry-go-round. Past the window, I hear my grandparents talking all mad in the kitchen. Past the carport and the family is stacking up some firewood for a fire. Past the window and Grandpa is saying something about how this is his house. Past the carport and the dad is down on the ground, burning up a little dry grass under the wood. Then it's Nana stacking away the dishes and getting rough with it. Then it's Vampi and her brother stealing a few tomatoes from the field and whoa—Xaman got a nice fire going. I stop the merry-go-round to have a good look. I love fires so much.

From her sack, the mom pulls out a brown grocery bag. She takes out an onion, dried masa for tortillas, eggs, and chorizo. Man, they have everything in those sacks! I'm watching the action when Grandpa comes out. He might still be mad, so I know I'd better get back on the bike to stay out of his way. He takes his hoe and heads out to his garden. I keep on riding around and watching Vampi's family.

They water the corn masa mix with water from the hose. Vampi begins rolling out the masa in a little plastic bowl. She looks nice now that she had her bath and fixed her hair and washed her feets.

Grandpa returns from the garden and in his hands, he has little baby zucchinis, which are not my favorite food, but one of my favorite words. The zucchinis have big yellow flowers on them, and it almost looks like he's trying to be some kind of Romeo when he gives them to Yuritzi. She smiles and says gracias. The dad says, "I know we're a bother. We're grateful to you for letting us stay. We'll leave soon."

"We're glad to help," says my grandpa. "But you can't stay long in this carport. It's not good for you with children."

"I know, señor. I know it's not good." They're both quiet for a moment, then Grandpa says, "I'll go and talk to the jefe right now. I think he can help you with some work."

"We hope so, señor. We're ready to work. We'll do anything. Grandpa gets in the truck and closes the door. He rolls down the window and asks me if I want to go with him.

"No, Grandpa, I'll play on my bicycle." He leaves, and I stay. The mom has the frying pan real hot now, and she drops in the onions and the chorizo. The breakfast smell is so good and chorizo is my number-two favorite smell after peanut butter. They're getting excited now, talking and laughing even, except I can't understand what they're saying. Sometimes I hear Spanish— "chorizo" or "trabajo," but then it is not Spanish at all. I have never heard this language. She cracks the eggs and they land in the red chorizo like six suns. She pops them and the yellow goes everywhere, and she stirs it all up. She looks at me and smiles. I smile too. Finally the chorizo is done and they take it outta the fire. Vampi's been making tortillas like crazy, throwing the masa from one hand to the other until they look nice and round. She's flipping them with her fingers, and they look good. Dang. Vampi's a good cook for a little kid. I tried making tortillas once, and mine came out all lumpy and shaped like shoe bottoms.

When the food is all made, they begin rolling little egg and chorizo taquitos with their hands. They lick their lips and their fingers even. It looks really fun, like camping. I smile at the mom again, and she smiles back. She rolls a taquito and passes it to Vampi. They talk their language, so I can't understand. Vampi stands up and walks over to me. She takes my hand and puts a little chorizo taco in it. I can see her little bat teeth when she smiles.

"Thank you. Gracias," I say. I take a bite and it's so tasty I have to take another before I'm finished with the first one. We all start laughing, cuz it's good and everybody knows it. I'm about to finish it off when Nana calls to me.

"Niño!! What are you doing?"

"They gave me it, Nana."

"Get in here. Now!"

"Señora, we are happy to share with him," says the mom. "We have plenty."

"Gordo, get in here now," says Nana again.

*   *   *

35

I go into the house. She looks like she can't decide if she's gonna cry or shout.

"You took food from them?"

"Yes, Nana. They gave it to m—" WHAM!! She slaps me across the face. She has never hit me there. We look at each other's faces. I can't believe it. She looks like she can't believe it either. I feel like I'm gonna cry, but I know everybody gets mad at me when I cry, so I don't.

"Can I go now?" I ask.

"Go," she says. I go to the living room and turn on the TV. It's the stupid news. I don't care. I lay on the sofa with my face in the crack. I hear the family laughing and eating outside. I hear Nana in the kitchen. I try not to move or make any noise, but I can't help it. The wet rolls down my cheek and into my mouth. I taste tears and egg and chorizo.

Cookie

Fat Cookie takes a tiny yellow library pencil out of her pants pocket. She looks from one side of the camp to the other, like a spy. She stares at the white wall in front of her like it's something interesting: a television show or one of those flea market posters of the most beautiful unicorn with a gigantic tail, running in the wind. With the back of her hand, Fat Cookie wipes a dusty spiderweb off the wall and then holds the tip of her pencil against the wall.

"What are you gonna do?" I ask her. She breathes.

"I'm thinking."

"Are you gonna write on the wall?" I ask. "Because if you do, you're gonna get in trouble with—"

"Shut up, idiot," she says to me but not in a mean voice, just tired, like a mom.

"Gordo, what do you even know about trouble?" she adds. "You don't have enough imagination to get into trouble. You're too busy kissing ass and reading your books."

"Fat Cookie, all the buildings in the camp belongs to Gyrich Farms. Even the outhouses. Besides, people live in this building, dummy. Tia lives there. Don Ramon. Heck, I'll bet it's against the law to write on that wall. You can't just grab your pencil and draw—"

"Maybe *you* can't, but I can, and I will. And don't call me Fat Cookie, cuz you're a fatty too." Cookie puts her big moon face right up to mine. I can smell her.

"You always smell like peanut butter," I tell her. "Is that all you ever get to eat at your house?"

"No. Sometimes we get the big block of cheese or the giant cans of tuna or chicken meat. What do you care anyways, you jealous?"

"No. Your mom can't even cook good," I say. "I saw her throw some meat in Wonder Bread and call it a taco. Meanwhile, my mom makes good food all the time. Fresh tortillas, pancakes, carne asada, pozole, chicken soup. Dee-licious."

"That all you ever think of, food?"

"No."

"Well it looks like it. I'm trying to start my drawing now, so shut it or I split your lip."

"Go ahead and try, Cookie. You split my lip and—"

"You'll what, bozo?" she asks.

"You split my lip and I'll kick you," I say. "Probably in the pussy!" Cookie wrinkles up her nose, like she smells something bad.

"In case you don't know," she says, "it doesn't really hurt that much if you kick a girl down there. All it'll do is make me mad, and then I'll have to kick you in the coconuts. If you got any. See if that finally shuts you up."

"You think you're so big," I say.

"That's cuz I am. I'm five years older than you. I'm taller than you and all the little punks on this ranch. In a year or two, I'm gonna start driving and get the hell out of here. For now though, I have to live here, and to be honest, I'm the queen of the Gyrich Farms Worker Camp. I'm a Chicana, not a beaner like you."

"What's that?"

"Being a beaner means you don't have papers to be in the USA. It means you're a mojado, just another wetback."

"No sir. I'm not no wetback. I was born over in Hollister, at Linda Hawkins Hospital. We've lived here in San Juan Bautista since I was a baby."

"What about your mom and dad?"

"They have their papers."

"They work in the fields," says Cookie. "They don't speak English. They live in this shitty camp with you. You think they got papers? No way, José."

"Well you and your mom live in the camp, and you got your papers."

"We're Chicanos. We're real Americans, not beaners. We belong here forever. Nobody can take us away to Mexico. We can speak English and we can write it too. We're not going to be in this shitty camp forever. My mom says we're leaving as soon as things get better. Maybe to Hollister or Watsonville, to live by the beach. We're going back to a real house with a yard, flush toilet, telephone, and no beaners."

"I'm not a wetback, and you ain't no queen, and what are you going to draw?"

"Shhhh," she says. "I'm an artist, mongoloid. I need quiet to do my work, so shut it."

Fat Cookie stares at the wall, moves her head from one side to the other. Then she takes her pencil and draws a big, perfect circle on the wall. Then she draws these little curved lines coming out of the circle, and they're the same size, same curve, same distance apart. It almost looks like they were made by a perfect drawing machine.

"Are you drawing the sun?" I ask. She doesn't even look at me. She stares at the wall. With her eyebrows all bunched up, Cookie looks like she's going to call out the wall to a fight, meet it after school behind the baseball field, and show it who runs the show.

She draws some more, and then I can see it. A pretty flower is growing right on the wall. Then she draws another flower that's hiding behind the first one. She draws two more big ones, and lots and lots of tiny flowers all in a bunch like grapes. Then Cookie begins drawing little marks inside of the petals.

"Stop drawing right now, Cookie," I say. "They're super good now. If you do anything more, you're gonna ruin them."

"I'm not gonna ruin them. This is what they call shading, tonto. You do shading to make them look more better, more prettier. Besides, they're my flowers. I can ruin them if I want."

She draws a little more, and it's true, she made the flowers more prettier than ever. Cookie draws teeny teardrops on the petals. They look so real, I can hardly believe it. She sketches curvy stems with little thorns. I want to tell her that only roses have thorns, well, roses, nopales, and other cactus. But I don't want to get her mad again, so I shut up. She draws jaggedy leaves on the stems and shades them in so they look like they're opened in the middle like a book, with veins.

Wow. This drawing is so boss. I always thought Fat Cookie only knew how to be mean. But she's not only mean, she's an artist.

Cookie outlines a ribbon under the flowers, but it's not some boring ribbon. It's all curved toward you in the front, then in the back it gets all twisted and the shading on this is the best ever. It's been a while, and my feets are getting tired, and I think maybe I should go home. But I can't stop watching. Cookie says, "Almost there." She writes "CHICANO POWER" across the ribbon in cholo letters that look like chino letters at the Golden Dragon, but they're not.

Cookie stops and steps back and stares at the drawing with me. Everything is floating. The flowers, the ribbon, floating in the air like the Virgin of Guadalupe.

"Wow, Cookie. I didn't know you were a artist."

"I just like to draw."

"You're a artist."

"You think so? Thanks. That's a nice thing to say."

"Yeah, man. Do your mom and dad know you can do this?"

"My mom hates my drawing. She says I'm becoming a chola, asks me why I can't draw nice things, the Virgin, ponies and shit. Fuck her."

"That's not cool, Cookie, what you said about your mom."

"Fuck her," she says again, this time in a louder voice.

"She brought you into the world, pendeja. She made you in her stomach and pushed you out of her vaginus. That's a fact. She gave you life, the greatest gift in the solar system."

"So what?" says Cookie. "Solar system. Pfft. You're the only idiot I know who talks about the solar system. You're so weird, Gordo."

"And what about your dad? Does he know you draw like this?" Cookie turns her head so fast, her braid whips around, as if somebody had slapped her.

"Fuck my dad too, wherever he is," says Cookie. "Also, Manny's not my real dad, idiot. He's only twenty-two. He's not even a stepdad. Manny is just another creepy boyfriend my mom found."

"I think Manny's nice," I say. "He gave me a ride in his Camaro, and that car is so fast. We drove all around the tomato fields, then to Lejano Market, and over to San Juan

Bautista going ninety all the way. One day, I want to have a haircut and mustache like his."

"You like him so much, maybe you should marry him, Gordo."

"All I'm saying is that he's nice."

"Sometimes he's nice. Sometimes he says nice things to me. Buys me nice things. But to tell the truth, that Camaro is the only really nice thing about him. He's a creep with sweaty hands. I need to finish this drawing."

Cookie draws one more leaf and steps back from her art.

"I think it's done now. What do you think?"

"I think that's really good art."

"Thanks, Gordo." She puts away her pencil and starts to walk away.

"You coming?" she asks.

"No," I tell her. "You're too mean today."

"I'm not too mean. You're too soft."

"No, to tell the truth, you're always mean."

"Okay, Soft Serve, don't hang out with me if you don't want to. I'll catch you on the flip side."

"Later, Fat Cookie."

"Fuck you, boobie man."

"Fuck you to infinity," I say.

"Fuck you more."

"Damn, you're stupid," I say. "You can't fuck more than infinity. Infinity is the end of the road. Maybe if you read some more books, you'd know that."

She walks away, holding both her middle fingers up in the air.

"Hey, Fat Cookie," I say. Cookie turns around, still giving me the double birdies. "In case you don't know. You're a crappy artist." Cookie opens her mouth like she's gonna say something mean, but instead she throws her pencil at me and walks away. I pick up the pencil. Dang. I wished I hadn't called her a crappy artist, but she is so mean. Now I can't tell her I'm sorry because if I say that, she'd win.

I look at Cookie's flowers. Half an hour ago, there was nothing on the wall, only paint and dusty spiderwebs. Now flowers. I think art is kind of weird. Those flowers came from somewhere, right? They weren't in the wall. They weren't in the pencil. They were in her all along. I picture Cookie stuffed with flowers from her toes to her throat, like a piñata. All those flowers in her, waiting to get out.

I'm looking at Cookie's masterpiece when WHAM, I get hit across the back of the head! I look behind me, and it's Tia Sara from next door with a broom in her hands.

"Ouch, tia! Why'd you hit me? I didn't do nothing."

"Nothing? Last time I looked, that wall was clean. Now, it has cholo drawings on it, and you're standing here with this pencil. What am I supposed to think?"

"I didn't do that drawing. Did you see me do it?"

"No. But if you didn't do it, who did?" Tia Sara looks at me all angry. She's not my real tia. We call her that because she and my ma are really good friends. She's really nice when she isn't swinging that broom around.

44

"I know you're lying, *Gordo*."

"No, tia, I'm not telling a l—"

"*Silencio*. You're going to tell me who did this, or I'll have to talk to your father about this. Was it Cesar?"

"No. Wasn't Cesar."

"Was it Cookie?" she asks. "There's another demon, just as bad as Cesar and twice as fat."

"I don't know who did it, tia."

"That Cookie is bad news," says tia. "But I guess it's not all her fault. With a mother like that, a girl can't be no good. Cookie thinks she's a grown woman, and her mami acts like she's a teenage girl, with that skinny plucked-chicken boy she calls her boyfriend. She thinks it's cute to have this young boyfriend, but it makes her look even older and more run-down, running with that pimply boy. Pfft. Can't even grow a good mustache yet. Now tell me, did Cookie do this?"

"Yeah. It was Cookie," I say.

"I knew it. Nasty child. Always cussing and shaking her maracas like they're something special. Drawing this mierda on the walls. I'm going to get her for this."

"Tia, if you tell Cookie I told you, she'll kill me."

"If she kills you, I'll kill her. And you should be glad I don't tell your dad so he can kill you too. Also, Gordo, don't lie to me ever again. I was married to a drunk for seven years. You think I don't know a lie when I smell one?"

"Okay, tia. I won't."

"And stop by the house right now. We've been work-ing the cucumbers at Calcano Farms, and we got some beautiful fresh ones to share. Take a bunch home to your mami."

The next day is Monday, and Cookie doesn't show up for school. I'm relieved I don't see her because I'm sure she is going to be mad at me. On Tuesday she's absent again, so I get to live one more day. It's good not to get hit, but I worry that Cookie is going to jump me, punch me in the head with those big fat rings on her big fat fingers. Could happen. That was why she got thrown out of San Benito Junior High, jumping a girl after school. I should probably try to hide from Cookie, but I'm curious and I want to know what is going on with her. No one has seen her for two days. Right before it gets dark, I pass by Cookie's house to see what is happening. I don't see Cookie, her mom, or Manny's Camaro. Everything is quiet. I go home and eat my dinner. I wash my dishes, and while I'm drying my hands, it gets very noisy. Everyone in the camp probably hears the screaming from Cookie's house. My sister, Sylvie, zooms out the front door of our house and stands behind our station wagon to listen. I go and stand next to her. At first I think that Cookie is getting busted for drawing on the wall. But no, it's not that.

"That's what happened," says Cookie. "I swear to God!"

"Well that's not what he says, and you can stop your damned lying now because I don't believe you, Cookie," says her mom, louder and louder. "Spent my whole pinche life taking care of you and now this. How could you? I'll never trust you again!"

"Then don't trust me, Mom! Go ahead and trust Manny, till he dumps you like all the other ones! Trust him so he can make you look stupid!" Then it gets really quiet in the house. Sylvie says to me: "Her mom's going to kill her." Next, we hear bad sounds. I know what they are—fighting sounds. Cussing. A body hitting a wall. A door slamming. Pounding on the door. The sounds of different things getting broken. Glass. Dishes. Maybe saints.

"I hate you so much!" screams Cookie. "I want you to die! Get away from me!" Then Cookie kicks open the screen door to the house so hard it slams against the wall and bounces right back into her chest. Her forehead is bleeding. She runs past me and Sylvie and shouts, "Fuck you all, fuckers!"

Cookie's mom opens the door. Her blouse is ripped at the sleeve and oooh, you can see some of her boob. She has a bloody scratch on her neck. Her hair is all over her face like a bruja's. She shouts at Cookie: "I worked for you since I was sixteen, Cookie! Worked the tomatoes, apples, garlic. You're gonna pay for that statue, cabrona!" Then she sees us behind the station wagon and tells me and Sylvie to get the hell out of her yard. Me and Sylvie go back into our house, close the door, and right away we start laughing. Maybe it's weird to laugh, but we don't know what else to do.

"Her *yard*?" says Sylvie.

"Oh my God, her yard," I say. "No grass. No fence. No flowers. Not even weeds."

"It's only dirt, and she calls it her 'yard.'"

We keep saying "my yard," and every time we do, we laugh more and more. Finally, we stop. I have tears on my cheeks. I clean my face. We both get serious.

"That was really bad," says Sylvie. I thought we'd seen all the fights. Fathers with mothers. Sisters with brothers. Fathers with sons, brothers, friends, neighbors, strangers. Friend fights. Cousin fights. Girlfriends and boyfriends. Dog fights. Cat fights. Roosters. Billy goats. But dang, I never even heard of a mother and daughter fight.

Two days later, Sylvie, Olga, Tiny, Cesar, and me are all hanging around by the canal. Cesar is using matches to try and burn a tire to roast some weenies for a feast when Cookie walks up to us with a big smile on her face. She looks pretty good. The bruise and cut on her forehead aren't too bad. Usually, Cookie puts her hair in a big braid, but today she is wearing it down. But the real surprise is the big smile on her face.

"Look what my mom got me, everybody." She is holding out a shiny red radio with a handle on top like a lunch box.

"Wow, that's nice," I say.

"It's a Panasonic," says Cookie.

"Does it work?" asks Cesar.

"Of course it works," says Cookie. "It's brand-new. My mom gave it to me."

"I thought your mom was mad at you," I say.

"She was. Then her stupid boyfriend, Manny, and her got in a big fight and I took her side and he left in the middle of the night and now me and mom made up."

"Does it play good music?" asks Tiny.

"Only the best music."

"Does it play 'The Hustle'?" asks Olga.

"Pssht. All the time. Every day I can hear 'The Hustle' five or six times. You guys wanna hear it?"

Everybody thinks it's a good idea. Cookie says, "C'mon then, let's play *American Bandstand*, over by the pump house. Bring your weenies. We can cook them with my lighter." We march out toward the pump. Cookie asks us what songs we hope we'll hear on the radio. It's weird that she is being so nice, but it's nice too. We make up our song list.

"'The Hustle'!"

"'Seasons in the Sun'!"

"'Tell Me Something Good'!"

"'Smokin' in the Boys' Room'!"

We're all getting excited until somebody says, "'I Honestly Love You.'" Most of the girls like that song, and I secretly like it too, but Cesar and Cookie hate it. Cesar starts singing "I Honestly Love You" like he's going to cry. Then he covers his face with his hands and howls like a wolf and everybody laughs because he is proving that the song is stupid.

At the pump house, Cookie goes to the ditch and pulls out a cattail. She uses the long stem like a giant pencil, drawing big squares in the dirt.

"What are you doing, Cookie?" asks Sylvie.

"I'm getting ready to start *American Bandstand*."

"How do you play *American Bandstand*?" I ask.

"Everybody has to dance, but you have to stay in your box. I'll be the judge and pick the best dancer. The most best dancer will get a special grand prize. Okay? Now get in your squares and I'll play the music. Only the best dancers will have a chance, so you better shake it till you break it."

Cookie clicks on the radio. It's some boring dude talking. Boo! She changes the channel. We hear cumbias. Boo! Country music. Double boo! Finally, she gets to Big Daddy Mario V. on KTOP. He's doing the Top 40! Cookie cranks the volume all the way up.

The first song we hear on the countdown is song number five, "The Locomotion." Yaay! Everybody cheers.

"Dance, you kids!" shouts Fat Cookie. We freeze. Nobody wants to be the first one to dance.

"I said dance, retards, dance!" shouts Fat Cookie. Then we start to giggle. Fat Cookie walks up behind Sylvie and smacks her in the head. That was a professional slap. You could really hear it.

"Dooooon't!" cries Sylvie.

"Well, then dance. All of you, DANCE!" We start dancing. I'm trying to look cool, but I'm not sure how. Tiny is still clowning around and dancing silly. Cookie goes up to her and kicks her in the ankle." Tiny crouches down, rubbing her ankle.

"Ooooooouch!" says Tiny.

"This is not a game," says Cookie, bending down so her face is right above Tiny's. "This is *American Bandstand*." Then we get dancing, and Olga is obviously the best. Fat Cookie watches her and says "Pretty good!" whenever Olga does a fancy step. When the song is over, everybody claps. Cookie says, "Round one winner and heavyweight champ is Olga."

Olga shakes her hips at us and we clap. Big Daddy Mario V. starts talking about song number four. He tells us how it climbed seven spots in one week, and everywhere he went to DJ, everybody asks for him to play it. In Watsonville, Hollister, Gilroy, they all want . . . "Kung Fu Fighting"! Oh yeah! For a long time, this has been the number one greatest favorite hit of all the kids at the camp. We hear the flute at the beginning, and as soon as the singing starts, we begin kung fu fighting, jumping and punching and kicking and going "Huah!" when the song goes "Huah!" The competition is tough now. I'm dancing hard and the sweat is getting in my eyes. I wipe it away and keep on dancing. I feel like I'm in a cool kung fu movie, like I have the five fingers of death and the thunder kick. Huah! Fat Cookie is cheering and laughing. It's so cool when she's not shouting or hitting.

"Good job, everybody!" shouts Cookie. "Tiny, stop copying everybody and make up your own steps. Keep dancing, everybody. This is better than *American Bandstand*! This is MEXICAN AMERICAN BANDSTAND!" Everybody goes

"Woo woo!" and "Awright!" and "Right on, sister!" and we all clap. Cesar is rocking out, man. He is dancing outside of the dirt square and moving through the group. His fists and feets and bony elbows are kung fu'ing all over the place. He pushes out his lips and looks at everybody all suspicious out the sides of his eyes, like Bruce Lee. He pretends he's dancing with nunchucks, and it looks so real that we circle around him and start cheering. The song finishes, and we're all breathing like we had just finished a race.

"This is a very hard decision," says Cookie. "There are many champeen dancers here at Mexican American Bandstand, but the winner is . . . Cesar!" Cesar pumps his arms in the air. He does a quick double kick and bows to the clapping.

"Now, it's time for the grand prize," says Cookie. "Winner takes all." She holds up a big, shiny coin.

"Fifty cents? Wow," says Sylvie.

"That's right," says Cookie. "This is for the big prize." Next on the countdown is song number three. It's "Rock Your Baby." I like this song. Everybody looks happy to dance, but Cookie starts complaining again.

"No! Not like that, you guys! Listen to the song. You have to dance with *soul*. Put some *soul* into it!"

"'Dance with soul'?" says Cesar. "What does that mean?" Cookie squeezes her head with her fingers to show that we're giving her a bad headache.

Then Cookie steps in and she starts to dance. At first, she looks kind of goofy, hardly moving at all. Her head is down. Her hair is hanging in front of her face like a black curtain.

She's listening. Then something changes. Cookie lifts her big round face to the sky. Her hair falls back, and she begins to move. Wow. The way she dances. It's pretty. It looks easy, like she's not even trying. She never looks at her feets. Her hips and shoulders go with the song, like she belongs to it. At the end of the song, the voice of the dude who sings it goes really high, like a girl's. Cookie's hands start drawing butterflies in the air. Is this soul?

When the song finishes, we all clap.

"Okay guys," says Cookie. "Show's over." She goes to her radio and shuts it off.

"What about the prize? Who won the fifty cents?" asks Cesar.

"I did," says Cookie. "I danced better than anybody. I'll see you kids later. I gotta go, I've got a big life to live." Cookie picks up her radio and walks back toward the houses, moving her hips and swinging her hair. As she walks away, a bunch of us flip her off. She doesn't even turn to see it.

"She thinks she's so big, but all she is is a big cheater," says Sylvie.

"She thinks she's better because she tricked us, but she's not," says Cesar. "All she is is fat and dark and mean and kind of ugly. But she did dance good." We laugh because it's true.

The next morning, Cookie doesn't show up at the school bus stop and we don't see her at school. After school, I decide to spy on her house to see what's going on.

"Sylvie, go with me to Cookie's house," I say. "Maybe she's sick or something."

"I don't wanna go. Her mom is mean. Remember what she said to us the day of the fight? She hates us. Besides, our ma said not to talk to her."

"You don't have to say nothing to her," I say. "I'll do all the talking. Don't you wanna know what's happening with Cookie? If you go with me, I'll let you look at my new *Archie* comic. C'mon."

"Hmmm. Okay, I'll go with you." She goes with me and we knock on the door. Nobody answers the door, but we can hear *The Price Is Right* on TV, so we knock some more. Nobody answers, so we knock harder.

"All right, all right!" says Cookie's mom from inside. I hear her moving in there, and it's kind of scary to hear her walking to the door. She opens the door. Wow. We can see and smell that the kitchen is wrecked. Dirty dishes and cans of Olympia Beer lined up on the counter. For once, she was wearing a normal mom nightgown instead of a mini skirt. Her face looks really different with no makeup.

"What do you kids want?" she asks.

"We came to see if Cookie wants to come play with us, maybe listen to music on the radio."

"Play with you?" she asks. Yeesh! Cookie's mom smells like a dad coming home on a Saturday after disappearing since Friday.

"Let me tell you something, Gordo. Cookie plays with boys all right, but not the little ones like you."

54

"Is she okay?" asks Sylvie. "She wasn't at school."

"She's not okay, and she's probably not gonna go back to school. She thinks she's too grown-up for school. Tell you what. If you kids see her and that punk Manny, tell them to give me back my radio and that I'm glad they're gone!"

"Okay, I will," I say.

"Is that all you kids want?"

"Yes that's all," says Sylvie. "We thought we would see Cookie."

"Too late for that. Won't see me either in a little while. I don't belong in this camp, and I'm going someplace nicer. I've got a big life to live. Goodbye, you two," she says.

"Goodbye," says Sylvie. Suddenly, the face of Cookie's mom changes, and her voice changes too, and she's really nice. She looks at Sylvie and says, "Mija, you got such pretty green eyes. You're as pretty as a gringa. Boys are gonna love you."

She looks at me and touches my hair. "Nice curls, mijo. I'd kill for curls like these," she says. I pull back my head. She reaches again, and I step back.

"Remember," says Cookie's mom. "If you kids see Cookie and Manny around town, tell them what I told you, okay?"

She steps back inside and she is about to close the door, but suddenly she stops.

"Hey, one more thing," she says.

"What's that?" asks Sylvie.

"Always be nice to your mom."

"Okay," I say. She closes the door on us. We walk away and I whisper to Sylvie. "That was weird."

"Yeah, it was," says Sylvie.

"You think we'll ever see Cookie again?"

"Yes," says Sylvie. "We'll see her around. I don't think she's gonna go far."

The Nasty Book Wars

When you leave a grapefruit on a countertop for a couple weeks, the membranes and fruity ligaments that hold together that nice rounded shape slowly weaken. Gravity insinuates itself, and the citrus's bottom begins a relentless downward migration. The underside spreads and takes on the flatness of the counter, while the top thins out. That defeated grapefruit shape was precisely the shape of Primitivo Doblado's head. Primi, as everyone called him, was a summertime fixture in the sunblasted garlic fields of Gyrich Farms. No one knew how he first arrived or how the lucky bastard managed to get hired as a garlic topper summer after summer when better workers were turned away by the proverbial truckload.

"How does he have the luck to get hired? I'll tell you how," my nana Lupita would explain. "In his wallet, Primi carries hairs from the ass cheeks of Satan himself. The luck of the Devil is with him. He is protected. No matter how he works, smells, or drinks, he'll keep getting hired."

By late July, the garlic had been pulled from the dirt and heaped in the fields, where it dried in the baleful San Benito County sun like mounds of tiny skulls. The stoop labor was performed in afternoon temperatures that hovered in the low nineties and sometimes more for weeks at a stretch. For this reason, summer was a season of dread to all the children age five and up, who harvested garlic alongside their parents. The worst day of school was better than the best day in the garlic fields, which to my child eyes stretched impossibly to the hazy edges of the Gabilan Range foothills, gold with paper-dry grass. My sister, cousins, and I were nothing special for working. In the early and midseventies, labor laws had not tightened up in farm counties, and children were commonly brought in to help with summertime harvesting. It saved on childcare expenses and added to the farm family incomes.

The workday started early, to beat the heat. Getting out of bed at sunrise was hard for kids and adults alike, but for Primi, it was unthinkable. He rarely made the 6:00 a.m. start on time or sober. Didn't have good hands, either. Shaky. His fingers were sunbrowned and clumsy, wrapped in filthy white medical tape to protect the many cuts he had self-inflicted with his garlic shears.

He had bulldog magic, Primi did, though, that charm of the grotesque. Quick to smile but no fucking neck. *Nada*. His head, jowly and big lipped like an Olmec idol's, sat squarely on his collarbones. To look to the sides, he had to turn his entire torso. Primi was a beer guy and looked it. A riverine network

58

of dilated capillaries marred his cheeks and perennially swollen nose. His beer gut jutted imposingly over improbably scrawny legs.

Everything about Primi seemed to invite teasing and mockery. Fortunately for him, he was unflappable and emotionally indestructible, able to absorb levels of mockery that would fell a lesser mortal, and funny enough to dish it right back. This created an entertaining and virtuous cycle of insults and comebacks that livened up the tedium of the workday. One afternoon, Primi fell asleep while enthroned in the porta potty toilet. His drinking buddy El Cuatro heard him snoring from a distance and called forth a trio of workers who stopped their labors and gathered around to laugh, jam the door with a stick, and throw dirt clods at the plastic walls as Primi cursed them from inside and pounded the walls, a cantankerous genie demanding release.

Primi had no wife to enforce grooming. The more forensically inclined garlic toppers studied his queerly angled bangs and sideburns and deduced that he had been cutting his own hair with garlic shears or a perhaps a bread knife. At lunch, Primi ate like a twelve-year-old boy blowing his allowance—Laffy Taffy, Cheetos, pickled pig knuckles, and Rainbo white bread sandwiches with triple baloney, double slices of American cheese, and, peeking out from underneath the meat stuffs, representing the vegetable kingdom, what might once have been lettuce.

The oracular musings of Primi were a source of fascination. The workers would lob questions at him.

"Primi, you wanna get married? Don't you want a wife?"

He mulled over the questions like an ascended guru.

"No, *ese*. I don't have money, so I couldn't attract someone better looking than me. I'd have to stay in my own league. Imagine a woman with looks like mine. No. No marriage. Besides, it's cheaper to rent."

"Primi, what's the best beer?"

"Whichever one is in my hand, loco."

"Primi, why do dogs love humans?"

"If you gave me free cans of food and cleaned up my *caca*, I'd love you too, homeboy. Woof."

When Ligo and conspicuously pregnant Chelo had an August wedding, they invited Primi and scores of other garlic toppers. The weddings of the poor are often anything but poor. They function as working-class Oscar nights, a rare avenue for glamour. The young women were unrecognizable out of their dungarees, work boots, straw hats, and sun-blocking sleeves. Their hair cascaded about their pale, exposed shoulders. Their painted lips left red marks on the lips of cups. The men did the opposite, covering up to mark the occasion. They covered their tanned forearms and necks in long-sleeve collared shirts. Tidied up their mandatory mustaches, draped their necks in gold crucifixes and chains. My eyes were most drawn to handsome Chulis in his slacks, worn tight as a tourniquet, at once concealing and showcasing his thighs and sundry goods. I could not yet understand why I was riveted so, but neither could I stop gawking.

*   *   *

Primi loved a party. He splurged and rented maroon Bosto-
nian lace-up shoes and a matching tuxedo with ruffles that
cascaded down the equator of his beer belly, making him
look like a downwardly mobile rain forest rooster puffing up
his plumes for one last mating dance. When he stepped into
the San Juan Bautista VFW hall with a living, breathing, live,
and unknown female escort, everyone whistled and catcalled.
He took it all in like the pope, bowing slightly to the left, the
right, and the center of the hall. For Primi, she was a looker,
and the gal had personality. She didn't know anyone but was
social and sparkly, laughing and chatting with folks as soon
as she arrived. Her name was Anamaria and, like Primi, she
had arrived pleasantly tipsy and quickly got to finishing the
job. Primi made several rounds to the bar, returning with
multiple cups in each hand. He lined them up, and they
tossed them back, getting louder and looser with each drink.

When the DJ kicked off a set of cumbias with Rigo
Tovar's "La Sirenita," Anamaria grabbed Primi by the hand
and pulled him toward the dance floor. That cumbia was a
huge hit, an irrepressibly buoyant story song about a fellow
who goes swimming, impregnates a mermaid, fathers a cute
merbaby with her, is arrested by King Neptune and charged
with eating her as seafood on a Good Friday, and is sentenced
to death, only to be saved by the last-second arrival of his
mermaid with their merbaby. The dance stylings of Primi

and Anamaria perfectly matched the musical shenanigans of the song. Primi couldn't dance well, but he could dance committedly, wobbling like a purple top on the verge of tipping over but never straying from the rhythm, even when the syncopation got tricky.

At our table, my pa watched the couple on the floor with a faint smile that I understood to convey affection and amusement. He raised his beer to them as they danced and shouted out encouragement for more, more, more from the couple. His excitement was contagious, and I also cheered them on, clapping and stomping my foot. Pa was possessed of an alchemical Mexican genius for transmuting physical defects into nicknames. He broke into raucous laughter as Primi shook his beer boobs and gyrated his flat ass. Primi strutted to the left and right, stalking the equally animated Anamaria. Halfway through the cumbia, Pa christened Primi "Head and Shoulders" and announced the name in his bullhorn voice: "Orale Head and Shoulders, dance loco!" The name stuck. It had to, because it was perfect: slicing clean to an undeniable truth about Primi. Besides, Pa had a christening reputation to uphold. He was almost synesthetic at times, able to confect nonsense names that sometimes worked at the level of pure sound. Bucktoothed Chendo, with his voracious chewing patterns became Chaka Chaka. Pretty chubette Rosa became La Burbulina. The Durango shitkicker Javi became the Quadruped. There was El Cuatro, Barrilito, Chulis, so many nicknames, all undeniably right, like Head and Shoulders.

The men in the garlic fields were relentless on the Monday morning after the wedding, batting Primi's new nickname back and forth across the fields like a badminton shuttlecock. Some of the young men could barely pronounce his English nickname, but it was too delicious, too perfect, not to take a jab at Primi.

Head and Shoulders here.

Head and Shoulders there.

Head and Shoulders up.

Head and Shoulders down.

Until the novelty passed, it would have to be this way, and Primi knew it, so he patiently smiled through the ordeal, periodically insulting everyone's mother, like a good sport should. When I called him Head and Shoulders to his face by accident, he actually laughed, releasing a great cloud of beer breath into my face. I was being disrespectful. He could have cussed me out, probably even smacked me, not on the face but upside the head, with full approval from my parents. I liked him in that moment. Not for the beer breath but because he kept his cool.

Head and Shoulders's last day at the Gyrich Farms Worker Camp came within a week of the wedding. Three dark-green migra vans descended on the garlic fields right before the midmorning break. They braked hard, kicking up clouds of dust. Four Immigration and Naturalization Service agents in khaki uniforms exploded from the opened doors. It scared me when several young workers bolted. They seemed so adult to me mere moments before, so full of the bravado and that physical competence of young men, hefting bushel baskets of garlic onto their shoulders with thoughtless ease. In a moment, they had been stripped of that and had been made into prey, fleeing to hide underneath cars or behind the stacked crates of garlic. I panicked and turned wide-eyed toward my mother.

"Should we run, Ma, should we run?"

"What are you talking about? You're a citizen. You were born here. They can't take you away." I was not reassured by her words.

"What about you, Ma? You were born in Mexico."

"Yes. But I have my papers," she said. "Now mind your own business, and keep on working."

I watched as Head and Shoulders rose up slowly, calmly. He walked a few steps, then he began running. It wasn't even ten in the morning, but he had already sucked down two Coors tallboys and was working on a third, so he was wobbly. Lurching toward the tall cattails on the banks of the irrigation ditch, Coors in hand, he tripped over a clod. Primi sprawled on the ground, arms and legs spread out like the Carl's Jr. star. His beer shot forth a geyser of foam, but amazingly he *never* let that beer can go. Two INS agents surrounded him and one helped him up by the elbow. Primi stood, and with his free hand, he sheepishly dusted himself off. He exhaled slowly, his shoulders dropping and eyes turning dirtward as he emptied his lungs. Oh no. I looked at Primi, and he winked. He raised his beer can to his lips, tilted his head back, opened his throat, and poured in the pissy remains. Conspicuously pregnant Chelo cried silently as Head and Shoulders bent his back and entered the rear maw of the INS van. Ligo tilted his head, sucked his teeth, and intoned, "Oh well, at least he got to finish his Coors."

That evening, the foreman's wife, Clarita, cleared out Head and Shoulders's tiny rental room in the big house. We called it that because it was the only two-story building in the worker camp, with three little rooms on the ground floor and three little rooms on the second floor. The rooms all held a wardrobe, a chair, a twin-size bed, and a night table. Only the colorful calendars, family photos, and knickknacks differentiated them. Clarita packed his clothes into grocery bags in case he should return, looking sadly at his undershirts, stiff and murky gray from bad washings with colored clothes, insufficient detergent, and clearly no fabric softener.

"A man without a woman," she said to the empty room as she ajaxed his hot plate for the next tenant, "is a sad animal. Sad. Don't know how to take care of themselves. A wonder they can wipe their own *culos*."

From behind the big willow tree that fronted the big house, my older sister, Sylvie, my older cousin, Cesar, my little cousin, Tiny, and I surveyed the cleaning with a vulture's watchfulness. Clarita packed his radio, Sunday Stetson hat, coin jar, and a few other valuables into a box for safekeeping at her house. As soon as she left and padlocked the door, we circled around to the back of the big house. We studied the window. She hadn't locked it, but there was a window lock latch that would make it impossible to open it all the way. Cesar punched through the rusted screen, and pried the window open with his jackknife. It only opened a few inches, but it was big enough for me to push Tiny through. Once inside, Tiny opened the latch. I opened the window wide, and we all climbed in. We went right to work, rooting around the room, hoping to find a spare dime under the bed, or matches, or comic books, or candy, or beef jerky, or maybe even cigarettes.

Sylvie opened the double doors of the rough-hewn wardrobe, and she and Cesar peered into the interior. They gasped simultaneously.

"Oooooooh! Oh my God! Oh my God! Oh my God!" squealed Sylvie.

"What is it?" I asked.

"Oh my good God!" added Cesar. Together they dragged out a brown grocery bag filled to the top with nasty girl magazines. Jackpot! We swooped down on the bag, tearing it as we reached in to yank out nasty books. Each of us grabbed a handful and retreated from the others like wolves protecting their hunks of deer leg from the pack.

"Ooooooh," I chanted from behind my copy of *Cheri*. "You can see her guts." I turned the centerfold around so everyone could see the eviscerated blonde.

"Thass not her guts, stupid," snarled Cesar. "Thass her pussy." At thirteen, almost fourteen, Cesar was the oldest and our resident sexpert. Tiny, only seven, was as confused as I was.

"How come it's all hairy?" she asked. Cesar had had enough.

"You're a bonehead, Tiny! Get out of here! This isn't for little kids." Cesar shoved her toward the open window. Tiny became teary-eyed and pleaded her case.

"I was just asking how come iss all hairy. I let you in, so you can't throw me out."

"GET OUT, LITTLE BABY!" hollered Cesar.

"I'm gonna tell Mom," she threatened, her voice quavering. "And she, an' she, she's gonna kick your ass."

"All right, then," Cesar agreed. "Shut up and don't ask any more stupid questions."

"I'm just asking how come it's all hairy, that's all."

"Look, little baby," said Sylvie. "When women grow up, they get hair. When you grow up, you'll get hair there too."

"No sir . . ."

"Yes sir. Matter of fact, your mom has hair down there. A big ol' bush."

"No sir. She wouldn't have all that hair, would she?" asked Tiny.

"She has all kinds of hair," asserted Sylvie. "Probably down to her knees. Like it or don't." The revelation was too much for Tiny. She began to wail.

"All right, that does it," said Cesar. "You girls get outta here. We gotta take these books and put 'em someplace safe."

"They're not your books, you know," countered Sylvie. "I was the one who opened the doors of the closet."

"But I saw them first," countered Cesar.

"But I touched them first. And Tiny got us inside, and Gordo got her through the window, so we found them together, and they're everybody's."

"That's fair. There are lots of nasty books. We can share," I offered.

"God, what kind of sissy idea is that?" asked Cesar. "Don't you get it, Gordo? What do the girls want them for? These books aren't for girls, they're for MEN!"

"You're not MEN," shrieked Sylvie. "You're only BOYS, and the girls wanna look at the pictures too!" Teary-eyed Tiny nodded her head in agreement.

"These books belong to the boys," Cesar proclaimed. "And we're taking them."

"Yeah, the boys," I added, eager to redeem myself as a dutiful foot soldier in Cesar's eyes.

Suddenly Sylvie grabbed an armful of magazines and made for the window. Cesar grabbed Sylvie by the pigtail and pulled her back into the room, and they began to struggle. Sylvie dropped the magazines, and the both of them slid on the glossy paper. Tiny and I entered the fray, and there ensued a tremendous ripping of paper, yanking of hair and centerfolds and opportunistic biting. The girls were scrappy, but they were no match for Cesar's brutal rabbit punches and my size. In short order, we expelled them through the window and latched it behind them. For added effect, Cesar closed the curtains. Sylvie, with a bit of crumpled centerfold still in her clenched fist, rapped on the window with her knuckles.

"Open the window! Gordo, you know we should get to see them too!"

I panted for a moment, and I shouted back at her through the curtain. "These are for BOYS, Sylvie. Go find your own dirty books."

"There aren't any. So the boys have to share!!!" Cesar parted the curtains, stuck his face to the window, and brayed his evil laugh. Sylvie flipped him off with both hands, repeatedly stabbing the air with her middle finger for emphasis. Tiny tried to imitate the gesture but flipped us off with her ring finger instead, sending me and Cesar into paroxysms of laughter.

"We'll be back, idiots!" shouted Sylvie. "And we'll bring help!" Cesar and I collapsed on the floor, rolling around on our spoils like Scrooge McDuck writhing about in his vast vault of coins. Cesar humped the floor lasciviously, kissed the centerfolds, and laughed like the supervillian-in-training he was.

The giddiness passed, and Cesar and I organized the books into neat stacks and recounted the story of the battle, embellishing new details as we repeated the epic. An hour passed this way, with us flipping through the books, jumping on Primi's creaky spring mattress, drinking his Coca-Colas, and drawing cars, dragons, and naked girls on paper bags. Cesar made a plan for the safe transport and safekeeping of the porn for our and only our use. He drilled me repeatedly about the plan. Looting a stack of porn was titillating, but the actual bodies on offer were ultimately uninteresting, almost embarrassing to behold. I felt ready to go home.

"I'm ready to go home, Cesar. I'm getting hungry."

"You're always hungry, fat ass."

"Say what you want, but we need to get out of here. I'm going to check and see if they're out there, okay?"

"Go ahead," replied Cesar. I cautiously parted the curtains and peered into the encroaching twilight.

"Do you see the girls out there, Gordo?"

"Nope. I think they're gone."

"You know the plan, right?"

"Yes, Cesar. You only told me a hundred times."

"If you know it so good," said Cesar, "tell me." I sighed and began reciting the plan.

"We fill that cardboard box with some of Head and Shoulders's junk. I go out the window with the box and pretend it's the books. I hide the box under the front porch stairs. The girls will see me and think they know our secret hiding place, but really they won't, because matter of fact, you will have the real books in those pillowcases, and you'll hide the books in the tractor barn and tomorrow we can look at the books all day after church."

"Yesss," he hissed, shaking his head. "They'll never figure it out. It's perfect."

I slipped out of Primi's window and Cesar handed me the box. I made a big show of pretending it was heavy with magazines. I scurried to the front of the big house, unlatching

70

the little iron grill gate that led to the crawl space under the stairs. I pushed the box through the opening and squeezed in after it. As soon as I disappeared beneath the stairs, I heard running footsteps. Through a crack in the stairs, I saw Sylvie and Tiny. Had they seen me? Shit.

"Ooh, Tiny," said Sylvie theatrically. "There's something under the stairs. I think it's an animal."

"No, it's not an animal. I think it's Gor—"

"I think it's a wild pig. We'd better lock it in before it eats Daddy's tomato plants." Before I could scramble out from under the stairs, Sylvie closed the latch on the iron grill. Sylvie peered through the metal grill and smiled as I struggled to force it open.

"*Que feo!* It's one of those big fat wild pigs." I tried kicking the gate but it only hurt my ankle.

"You better let me out!" I growled.

"Ooh, the pig is mad, but he better not get too mad, 'cause Mami is right over there across the way in the kitchen and she'll come out if he makes too much noise, and she'll wanna know what you're doing down there, and we'll have to tell her all about the nasty books." I glared at her through the grill. She smiled serenely.

"You boys think we're stupid, but we're not. Right now Fat Cookie is kicking Cesar's ass and getting those books back."

"Fat Cookie can't beat Cesar up. He's tough."

"You think he's the baddest, but he isn't." It was true. I had no retort. Sylvie sprinted toward the tractor barn. My heart was pounding so hard I could feel it in my temples. I crouched beneath the porch for ten or perhaps thirty minutes. It is difficult to gauge that when you're doing hard time. I sat there hoping there were no rats or trapdoor spiders or bobcats or bears. Finally, Sylvie returned and, without ceremony, opened the latch. I sprang from the gate opening and tried twice to kick her, but she was way too fast for me. I jogged to the tractor barn, calling for Cesar. There I found him pinned, stomach down, underneath Fat Cookie, who was counting out loud, her fleshy lips slowly intoning each number.

"One hundred five. One hundred six. One hundred seven."

Fat Cookie's ambush had evidently been rough. Torn porno scraps were strewn about them. Cesar and Cookie were filthy from rolling around in the oily dirt of the tractor barn. Cookie had a little blood visible in her nostril. A long scratch ran across Cesar's arm. His shirtsleeve was torn. Fat Cookie had twenty, thirty pounds on him. He never stood a chance. In the face of defeat, Cesar remained a defiant POW.

"Those magazines are for men!" said Cesar.

"Not anymore," countered Fat Cookie. "I beat you fair and square for them, bozo. They're ours now, and we're taking them."

"You girls are stupid," said Cesar. "What do you wanna see naked girls for?"

"That's for me to know and you to find out. Now shut your trap and let me count to two hundred so I can finish your punishment and let you go."

"Fuckers," spit out Cesar.

"You guys are the fuckers," said Fat Cookie. "If you had only shared, we would all have magazines and I wouldn't have had to rack you up." Cookie looked at me, saw me trying to figure out what to do.

"Gordo, you're not stupid enough to think you can save this bozo, right? You know I'll rub his face in the dirt if you take one step closer, right?" I didn't say anything.

"You'd better get home, little boy. Or your buddy here is going to get it even worse." I looked to Cesar. He motioned me away with his head. I walked home in the darkening gloom, marveling at the totality of our defeat.

For the next few days, the girls demonstrated how far in advance they were in the realm of psychological operations and manipulation. They led Cesar and me on a ranging series of dead-end excursions. We'd spy the girls gathering behind the chicken coops and moving on purposefully to some unlikely place like the garbage heap or the inside of the abandoned Chevy that rusted away on the edge of the fields. There they would huddle tightly and converse with their backs turned toward us, hiding their faces and gestures. Cesar and I would descend on them with an "AHA!" only to find them empty-handed.

"Looking for something?"

"None of your business, Sylvie."

"Then why did you say 'aha'?"

"Just because."

"You'll never guess where we hid them, Cesar. You know why? Because we're smarter. We might wait fifty-seven hundred million days before we even look at 'em. We're patient." Mocking laughter lashed us as we retreated. Entire days passed, and we saw no signs of activity. I was rapidly losing morale and interest, but it had become a quest for Cesar.

"Gordo, I have a plan to get the books back."

"What's the plan?"

"Secret. But you gotta be in the plan or it doesn't work."

"What am I gonna do?"

"It's a secret, stupid. You do what I tell you, no matter what. Will you obey?"

"Umm . . . okay."

"First we gotta find Tiny."

"I think I saw her over by the trailer."

"Good. C'mon."

As we approached, we heard Tiny holding court at an al fresco tea party in the garden near a worker trailer. Kneeling in the dust, she served up mud pies and tin cans of water to her motley collection of rescue dolls. With their missing arms, hollowed-out eye sockets, scalped hair, and mismatched clothes, the dolls seemed to have crawled out of some horrible toy apocalypse, but Tiny didn't care. She was a stellar hostess, making chatty conversation with them and even serenading them with one of her patented fuck-up songs.

"Conjunction Junction, what's your fuck shuh? Lookin at worse and raisins in closets. Conjunction Junction, how's that fuck shuh? I got ants button or they get you pretty far."

"Oh, Miss Kitty, you look so pretty today," she fussed. "Would you like some more cake and tuna? How about some Dr Pepper?"

"Get her," snapped Cesar. I pounced from behind the trailer and grabbed Tiny from behind. She squealed and squirmed to escape but quickly saw there was no hope. Cesar assumed the role of inquisitor.

"Tiny, where are the nasty books?"

"I don' know," she said.

"Don't be stupid, Tiny. I know they told you to keep the secret, but you have to tell us, or we'll make you suffer."

Less convincingly now, she repeated her denial. WHAM! Cesar slapped her across the cheek. We were all silent for a moment, shocked at what had happened, trapped in the harsh unfolding of events that now seemed to be hurtling along with their own terrible momentum. Tiny opened her mouth wide. She was one of those delayed-howl kids who held their mouths open for eternities, sucking in great lungfuls of air before unleashing a deafening cry. Cesar raised his hand before her face.

"Shut up or I'll hit you and harder this time." Tiny whimpered and went silent.

"Cesar, this is bad," I said. "Don't hit her on the fa—"

"Shut up and stop being a pussy," countered Cesar. "Tiny's going to tell me where the books are. Aren't you, Tiny? Where are they?"

"It . . . it . . . it . . ." she faltered.

"Where?!"

"It's in the old refrigerator," she sobbed. "Over by the ditch behind the big house."

"Let her go. Next time, you don't take boys' stuff, Tiny."

"Maybe we will," she countered in a quavering voice. We were impressed by Tiny's spunk but laughed anyway. We had broken her. The gods of war were with us again.

The nasty books were stuffed into the meat and vegetable bins of the abandoned refrigerator. They smelled weird now, and many of the pages had tears, oily dirt, and dusty footprints from the ambush in the tractor barn. Still, our joy was expansive as we repacked the storied booty into a burlap sack. We had only a few minutes to act before Tiny rounded up the girls and found us. We grabbed a shovel from the tractor barn on the way to the tomato field. There, we hid behind the mammoth wheel of a tractor and began digging.

"This plan is perfect, Gordo. They'll never find our books now," grunted Cesar as he shoveled.

"Yeah, perfect." We buried the nasty books and headed back to the toolshed. On our way, the girls intercepted us but said nothing. They stared at us, disgusted and silent. We retreated, checking behind us all the way for some unexpected maneuver. It was eerie, that silence, those glares. Nothing happened, but it felt like even the most extravagant acts of revenge were possible now.

At home that night, I showered and drank my nightcap, Pancho Pantera chocolate powder mixed with milk. But I could not sleep. In the bunk above mine, Sylvie lay silent. I knew she was awake. I felt her contempt radiating through the bottom of her bunk, searing me from the inside out like microwaves.

"You asleep?" I asked. She said nothing.

"I told Cesar it wasn't cool to slap Tiny," I offered. She said nothing. We laid like that. She wasn't sleeping. I wasn't sleeping. Eventually I drifted off to sleep, enveloped in the malignant, suffocating quiet.

All the next day Sylvie maintained monastic silence. By dinner, Mom had become curious.

"Why are you two quiet?" asked Ma.

"It's nothing," I said. "We don't feel like talking."

"Don't tell me it's nothing. If you're not talking, something's wrong."

"I'm finished eating," said Sylvie. "Can I go now, Mami?"

"Yes, but if something serious happened, you need to tell me."

"No, nothing serious." Sylvie retreated to our little bedroom and closed the door behind her.

"Do you want the rest of Sylvie's chicken?" asked Ma.

"No thank you. I'm full."

"I guess this is pretty serious," said Ma.

"Just an argument," I offered.

Our war had escalated and taken on its own momentum. I didn't really care about the books anymore. I don't know if anyone did. It was now a war for the victory of boys or girls—an excruciating binary to a sissy boy like me. The chess game was foreboding. I wanted to tell Sylvie where the books were, but that would show Cesar I wasn't a real boy. Surely he would punish me, severing my tenuous connections to the world of boys. I would be exiled to the world of girls, and surely they would send me away too because I wasn't one of them or even a good enough ally to them. Troubled for yet another night, I counted sheep in the dark. Then horses. Deep into a chicken count, I finally fell asleep.

For three days, we let the books lay in the soil of the fallow tomato field. Troubled though I was, I still enjoyed exchanging conspiratorial glances with Cesar, to know the girls were baffled, to know the dirty books lay in the soil, awaiting their day like fleshy seeds. On the fourth morning at dawn, as we slept, a tiller tractor made its first pass over the field and the box of porn. All morning long, it crisscrossed the field, its great steel discs cleaving the soil, breaking it into ever-smaller clods with each pass. The dirty books did not fare well, and by the time we'd awoken and stepped outside, we could only watch helplessly from the edge of the field as the tiller scattered the slivered magazine pages across the dirt. Late summer breezes kicked up dust and centerfold remnants. My nana Lupita emerged from her kitchen to use the outhouse. On her way there, she saw a pink scrap of centerfold. It was, of course, the worst possible bit she could have picked up. She studied the photo through narrowed eyes and after a moment deciphered it. "Jesus, Maria, y José," she whispered under her breath. The Devil was hard at work, but she knew exactly what to do. Nana alerted the neighbor Doña Paquita, quarantined us in the house, and the two ran about like fussy hens, chasing down every scrap they could find and tossing it in a paper sack. The burning of our pornography was perfunctory and largely unmourned. We were war-weary and ready for a truce.

For weeks afterward, scraps missed by Nana and Doña Paquita would appear in corners—bits of tit, snatches of snatch, hanks of hair, and bouquets of tightly clenched toes that skipped along the dusty worker camp. Fat Cookie instructed everyone to grab every nasty scrap and collect them in a weathered cigar box that would serve as a reliquary. Periodically, we opened the box, laid the pieces out on a tabletop, and studied them with Talmudic intensity. We tried to piece together a proper nude, but could only assemble grotesque Frankenforms with outsized lips, mismatched limbs, and demented eyes that elicited not titillation but uncontainable laughter that swept us off the ground and tumbled the lot of us, like a perfect wave.

Fandango

W hoa. A gringo is coming to work in the garlic fields. I
see him first thing Monday morning, right as everyone
is about to start working. We are all putting on our gloves. My
grandpa is sharpening our shears. The gringo goes to the stack
of bushel baskets and takes one. He sees me looking at him
and smiles and waves. He is the reddest person I ever seen.
His hair is red, and his face is burnt red. Even his eyelashes
are red. Most of the garlic toppers at Gyrich Farms are Mexicans, like us. The women, the men, the kids. Heck, even the
dogs all have Spanish names, so they're sort of Mexican too.
That's why seeing a gringo here is surprising, like a Bigfoot.

My ma shouts, "Buenos dias, Juan Diego!" at the red
gringo. She and my pa wave and wave at him, with both
hands. The gringo acts like they aren't even there. He keeps
walking away, but then he finally notices them. His is mouth
drops open, his red eyebrows go up, his blue eyes open wide,
and he waves back.

"That gringo's name is Juan Diego?" I ask Ma.

"That's not a gringo, that's Juan Diego," says Ma. "And he's from Aguascalientes in Mexico, like me."

"He worked here at Gyrich Farms two, maybe three years ago," says my pa. "Then we never saw him again. Now he's back. That man is the fastest garlic topper you'll ever see."

"So he talks en Español?" I ask.

"No," says Ma.

"He talks in English?"

"No, Gordo," says Ma. "He doesn't speak English, doesn't speak Spanish. He's mute."

"What's that?"

"Juan Diego can hear, but he can't talk."

"Why?"

"I don't know, and we won't ask, because it's none of our business," says Ma.

"Some people have bad luck," says Pa. "Pobre Juan Diego. He was probably born that way. Maybe he got sick when he was little, and his tongue wouldn't work anymore."

"That's weird," I say.

"It's not weird, it's sad" says Pa. "Think how hard it must be to have no voice. To never talk."

After a few days of working with him, I see that Juan Diego does talk. Kind of. He has big ol' catcher's mitt hands with red hairs and freckles on the back, and if you watch his hands and face, you can sometimes figure out what he's saying. Every day when I see Juan Diego at work, he's nice to me. He smiles, he waves. I wave back and say, "Hola, Juan

Diego, how are you?" He smiles and sticks his thumb up to show he's doing okay. Then I stick my thumb up too. After a while, I can understand a bunch of the things he's saying.

Back of the hand across the forehead means: "Whew, it's hot."

Circles on the belly with his hand means: "Your lunch looks good. I'm ready to eat too."

Drinking from an invisible cup means: "I'm thirsty."

Dad was right. Juan Diego is fast. He's like the Flash with his hands. Snip, snip, snip! Fast, fast, fast! Stems and roots go flying when Juan Diego gets to work, and the garlic heads pile up in his basket like magic. Sometimes he tops more than forty bushels a day. I can do ten, maybe twelve if the garlic is big and nice and dry so the stems and roots are easy to cut. Ma is one of the fastest girls. She can do about twenty-five or thirty bushels a day. Pa does about the same.

At the worker camp, Juan Diego shares a little room with two brothers. The room is on the ground floor of the big house. The brothers are Benito and Manuel. They both look like they should be in high school, but Pa says they can barely read, even in Spanish. They always come to work at Gyrich Farms alone, with no mother or father. Everyone calls them Los Tigres, because they have greenish eyes. The brothers look like indios. They're very brown with shiny white teeth and super black hair. Ma guesses they're about sixteen or seventeen years old. I'm not even ten, but I'm as tall as both of them. Los Tigres are small, but they're tough. Manuel is the older one. He lifts weights, and he has a thick scar on his neck that looks like a fat caterpillar. Benito, the little brother, looks more normal and not so scary. Los Tigres are too old to hang out with us kids and kind of young to be with the men, so mostly they hang out with each other. But sometimes on Saturday nights, they hang out with the men.

One Friday after work, I pass their bedroom window at the big house, and I see them sleeping in their tiny bed with their shirts off. I stop and watch them. They're right next to each other, face-to-face. When they breathe, their chests go up and down at the exact same time. They're perfect twins, even if they're not twins. They're sleeping so hard I wonder if they started the weekend drinking early. Los Tigres are kind of famous for being champion drinkers in the camp. That's a big deal, because all the men at the Gyrich Farms Worker Camp drink on Saturdays like they've been walking through the desert all week to get to a Coors tallboy.

The Saturday night drinking fandango happens all summer when the garlic and tomato harvests are happening. After dinner, the men bring broken branches and scraps of wood to the tractor barn to start a fire. It's not even cold in the summer. I think they just like making fires. Once the fire gets going, the guys bring chairs from their kitchens: blue chairs, orange chairs, new chairs, ripped chairs. My pa had a big green easy chair that lives in the tractor barn under a big blue plastic sheet. Pa's chair looks like it got into a long fight with some bears. It has long rips in it, and you can see the dirty cotton sticking out. It has one broken leg, so it's kind of wobbly. But that ugly chair is my pa's throne. He loves it, and nobody else gets to sit there. When Pa goes to get his big chair, he rips off the plastic with both hands, like a magician uncovering a pretty girl. Then he drags his chair out into the circle, and he always parks it in the same spot, with his back to the wall, facing the entrance.

My Tio Hector brings his little red record player and albums. He plugs the player into a long extension cord connected to another long extension cord that goes into his kitchen window. My tio always carries in his stack of records, but to be honest he only needs to bring one, because most of the night they play one thing again and again. Vicente Fernández. Oh my God, it's always and forever Vicente. Vicente doing rancheras. Vicente doing boleros. Vicente shouting out the gritos. Ay ay ay! Vicente is the king of the drunk guys who are only happy when they're sad.

When all the chairs are out and the record player is plugged in, they need one more thing—the most important thing. Beer.

Everyone brings beer. Six-packs, tallboys, cases, big brown bottles like the hoboes drink by the train tracks. Olympia, Hamm's, Lone Star, Schlitz, and especially Coors. When one of the guys travels to Mexico, he always comes back with big ol' honking bottles of Tecate or Estrella. They call the big Mexican beers "caguamas," and everyone gets super excited and they pass the bottles around. The caguamas are special. I can tell because when they drink them, they close their eyes and they look so happy, like hungry babies with baby bottles. Then they go "aaaaah," like Tecate comes from heaven, instead of dusty old Mexico.

Tonight I decide to hang out with the men while they drink. Most of the other boys in the camp don't like to. When I told Sylvie I was going to the fandango, she asked, "Why are you going to hang out with those drunks? They're dangerous."

"Because I want to."

"This is a bad idea, bozo, but go ahead. You'll get what you get."

I grab a bucket, flip it upside down, and that is my throne. I sit outside of the circle, almost in the dark. I stay quiet. It's nice, like being invisible. When I try to stay for the fandango, Pa usually tells me to get out, but sometimes he lets me stay. Tonight, he lets me stay. Probably I shouldn't stay. Bad things happen at the fandango—not every time but a lot of the time. Some drunks are happy. Some are sleepy. Some are sad. Some like to sing. Some are angry. They're like the Seven Dwarfs; everyone's different. The problem is that some of the guys get mean or just need to fight. When they fight, it's exciting but really scary, like when you're watching Godzilla fighting a big monster and they're knocking down buildings, stomping on buses, and throwing around tanks. It makes you want to run like the people in Tokyo trying to get away from the monsters. Drunk guys are scary, and to be honest, I think the guys are kind of scary even when they're not drunk. Including my pa.

I remember once when Manuel scared me. He lifts weights all the time. He doesn't have money for real weights, so he has two paint buckets full of rocks and water, and he lifts those. He lifts them to the front, to the side, and behind his back. Sometimes his face looks like the lifting really hurts, but he keeps on lifting. I was walking home when I passed the big house. He was standing in front of his room lifting his buckets up and down. I started looking. He didn't have no shirt on. He had some hair on his stomach and on his chest. When he lifted his arms up, I could see the muscles popping up, big as a softball. I wasn't doing nothing to him, only watching, and he saw me, and he started mad dogging me. I was confused and thought, *Is he mad at me? Why is he mad at me if I'm only watching?* I kept watching him lifting the buckets and puffing out air like a little dragon. Then he stopped lifting weights and he came to me. He stood right next to me, angry. I could smell his chest, his breath. I froze like a possum on the road, about to get run over. He pulled back his fist and went to punch me, but he stopped his fist right in front of my face. I jumped back and tripped. I landed in the dirt, covering my face.

"What? You scared of me, Gordo?" he asked. He was smiling, but it wasn't a happy smile. "No answer? Well, you should be scared of me, Gordo."

"How come you're saying that? What did I do?" I asked him, but my voice came out tiny.

"What did you say?" he asked. I wanted to answer but my voice wouldn't come out.

"Speak up, Gordo. What's wrong with you? Why don't you speak up like a man?"

"Because I'm not a man."

"Then what are you?"

"A boy. I'm a boy."

"That's what you think," he said. Manuel hated me. I did something wrong, and I still don't know what it was, but it made me feel bad.

I walked away and turned the corner as fast as I could. I felt better once he couldn't see me. Becoming invisible would be the best superpower. I think that a lot of people don't like what they see when they look at me. I'm doing something wrong all the time, but I don't understand what it is. That's why I sometimes stay with the men on Saturday nights. They're normal. With them, maybe I can learn how to be a normal boy, a real boy, instead of me.

But do you know what else? I stay because the guys are really funny. Oh my God, they always have something funny to say about somebody, except my dad because he's scary and Big Rafa because he's Big Rafa. So many jokes. About El Cuatro's hairy ears and how he's really half rabbit. About Barrilito's big stomach and how he's gonna have a baby, no two babies, twenty pounds each, any day now. About Chulis's pretty face and big butt and how they want to marry him instead of his sister. When Chulis stands up to get a beer, they start with the kissing noises, and sometimes they pinch his butt.

"Why don't you go and grab your mother's ass instead?" says Chulis. And everyone laughs and loves it.

Some of these poor guys are like the chickens that get their head pecked all the time by the other chickens. Have you ever seen that? It's bad. A bunch of the chickens gang up on one chicken, pecking and pecking on the head and neck and back like it's their job. After a while, the poor chicken is almost bald or even bleeding, but they never stop pecking. I once saw a big red rooster pecking and pecking at this one little chicken. The little chicken was all bunched up, squatting in the dirt with its head down, but the rooster kept on pecking and pecking, like it wanted to kill the little guy.

I get picked on all the time for being fat, cuz I can't throw a ball, for speaking English all wrong. So when I saw that little chicken getting picked on, I got pretty mad at the rooster and came up behind it and kicked it as hard as I could. I got that fucker right under the ass and he flew up like a red football and he tried to fly, but instead he crashed on his side. The rooster stared at me, ready to attack.

"How do you like it when someone picks on you, fucker?" I asked the rooster. The rooster turned its head a little bit sideways like he was thinking, then he came running at me. I got scared and ran, and he was right behind me. Crazy rooster! I grabbed a mop from the porch, and swung at him. BOOM! I nailed him right on his side and he rolled two times. He got up. He tried to flap his wings, but only one came up. The other one didn't move.

"You wanna fight?" I asked him. He walked away with a bad limp. Shit. I really racked him up. I felt bad. Maybe I broke something. I kept thinking I was going to get it if the rooster died. I shouted at him, "Hey chicken! Don't die! And next time, don't be a bully!"

So the men start drinking, and after a couple of beers, Juan Diego leaves the circle and in a moment he returns with a big square bottle in his hand. He holds his bottle above his head and waves it around like a trophy. Everyone gets real excited, and they're calling his name. Chulis and Cuatro even make excited monkey noises.

"Monte Azul! My favorite!" says Cuatro. "Today we drink like kings!"

Juan Diego smiles, opens the bottle, takes a big drink, and passes it around. Everyone does the same, and they're so excited to be drinking this. They close their eyes and take big drinks, and then they let out air and shake their heads, like they can't believe it's so good. Wow, it must be so good. The bottle gets back to Juan Diego, and he stands up and brings the bottle to me, and he points at my chest and pretends to drink from the bottle.

"You want me to drink?" I ask him. He shakes his head and everybody starts laughing. I'm laughing too, like it's a big joke. But he keeps holding the bottle in front of me. I look at my dad, cuz I don't know what to do, and my dad nods his head a little at me, telling me to take a drink. Okay, I will.

I take the bottle and look at Pa again, and he's nodding and smiling. His eyes are shining. Everyone is quiet now. I grab the bottle with both hands, hold it up to my mouth, and take a big gulping drink, then two more. Juan Diego grabs the bottle from my hands and some tequila spills on my shirt.

Everyone is laughing and cheering! Some of the guys are standing and jumping up and down, pointing at me.

"That's my Gordo!"

"Caramba, un tequilero campeón," they say. When they see my face all scrunched up from the bad flavor of the tequila, they laugh some more. It tasted awful, but now everybody likes me. For once, all the guys like me! They joke and joke about my drinking, and I feel good. I move my chair closer to the fire. Cuatro makes room and tells me to sit next to him, so I do. He puts one arm around me. This is really nice. I'm in the circle now.

The guys drink some more, and they get louder and funnier and scarier. I think I'm a little drunk too because I'm giggling and giggling, and I can't stop. Then my Tio Hector gets up and flips the Vicente Fernández record on the record player. All the guys start singing along to "Volver, Volver" with their arms around each other, shouting gritos into the air. Louder and louder they sing the sad song about wanting to go back, back, back to her arms.

I look and I see that Juan Diego is crying. His face looks like he just broke a leg or something. It's the saddest crying I ever seen, because Juan Diego didn't make no noise, only a sound like air coming out of a small hole in a tire. Oh my God, I never seen a man cry so much. I feel myself start crying. I wipe my eyes, because I don't want them to see me crying, but it doesn't matter anyways because everyone has stopped singing and drinking. They're looking at Juan Diego.

Someone asks the group what's wrong with him. Tio Hector gets up, goes to Juan Diego, crouches down, looks him in the face, and puts his hands on his shoulders.

"What's the matter, Juan Diego?"

Juan Diego tries to tell the story of the tears with his hands. His hands begin to move all over the place. Sometimes they look like little man climbing up stairs, a bottle rocket flying up and exploding, a butterfly in the wind, a claw cutting him across his cheek. Juan Diego looks up, and he sees everyone is quiet and confused. Juan Diego starts punching his heart.

Boom.

Boom!

BOOM!

He hits himself harder and harder like he wants to crack open his chest and take out his sad heart. Tio Hector grabs Juan Diego's hand to stop him from hitting himself. Juan Diego's so damned strong he keeps on hitting himself, then my tio grabs him with both hands and makes him stop. He puts his face right up to Juan Diego's like he's going to kiss him, but he doesn't. Instead he talks to him real slow.

"It's okay, amigo mio. You can cry, but don't hurt yourself. Whatever happened, it's done." Juan Diego looks down. He opens his fist and stares into his hand. He puts his hand on his heart and begins moving his mouth like he's singing along with Vicente but with no voice. He tries to stop crying, but it comes out again, like a hiccup. Juan Diego looks down at the dirt, and his shoulders go up and down.

"Let it out," says Chulis. He's crying too. "Llorala, Juan Diego."

"Llorala?" I think. How does Chulis know that Juan Diego is crying for a girl and not something else? Juan Diego calms down. He sits up and takes a big drink from the Monte Azul bottle.

"You in love, Juan Diego?" asks Chulis. Juan Diego looks at him and he shakes his head no.

"You okay then?" asks Chulis. Juan Diego lifts his thumb into the air to show he is okay now. He grabs the bottle of Monte Azul and drinks the rest in three gulps. Then he burps, and everyone laughs, and he laughs, and everyone starts drinking and talking.

Suddenly, it's like we're all okay. I guess nothing happened.

"That's enough sad songs," says Tio Hector. He walks over to the record player and says, "Now let's have a party!" He looks through the stack and takes out an album. It's KC and the Sunshine Band! He starts playing "Get Down Tonight"! YES! I love that song! Some of the older dudes aren't too excited, but I am, and so are Los Tigres. They're smiling, with their eyes almost closed from drinking, and they're moving their heads back and forth and loving it. Benito, the little Tigre, stands up and starts moving his feet, then he leaves the circle, and he starts dancing. He's really good, and every step matches the music. Benito pretends to be dancing with a girl, holding her by the waist, kicking up all kinds of dust in the dirt with his feets. Disco at Gyrich Farms! He turns around and shakes his butt at everybody, and they love it so much and start laughing. Some of the guys stand up and start clapping. Then Manuel, the other Tigre, stands up. At first, I think he's gonna dance too, and I'm thinking it's gonna be great. But noooo, it's something else. Manuel looks really mad and he goes to his little brother.

"You call that dancing?" shouts Manuel. "You can't disco, puto! I tried to teach you, but you can't disco!" Benito don't care. He keeps on dancing. Then, Manuel starts dancing, and oh my God, he's really bad at it. He can't get down tonight or any night! He pumps his arms like he is weight lifting, and he thinks he's so cool, but everybody is laughing, like it's a big joke. Manuel's face looks angry. He looks again at his little brother. Benito is so smooth, so cool. He looks like he's dancing on *Soul Train*. Manuel's eyebrows get all mean like a bad guy in a comic book, and suddenly he runs and tackles little Benito. They both hit the dirt, and Manuel is swinging and swinging, nailing his little brother on the shoulders, neck, face. It's wild monkey fighting, man! I stand up to watch, and it makes me dizzy. I see Benito get out from underneath Manuel. He stands and faces Manuel. They're breathing hard, and everyone's telling them to stop fighting and settle down, but Manuel can't stop. He grabs Benito by the shirt and pulls him down to the ground. Manuel swoops down to punch Benito in the face, but Benito kicks up at him. BOOM! Benito's kick is perfect. He nails his big brother right under the chin with his work boot. Oh man! I can hear Manuel's mouth snap shut and his head pops back and he lands face up in the dirt. My pa says, "Son of a bitch!" really loud, then everyone gets real quiet.

I go over to Manuel and like a dummy I ask if he is okay. The guys circle around Manuel. He opens his mouth and inside it's like a cup of blood. He spits it all out and pokes his finger in his mouth.

"My tongue," he says. He can't talk right. Benito gets on his knees next to Manuel, takes off his T-shirt, and gives it to his big brother.

"Press this against your mouth," says Benito. Manuel takes the shirt and does that. Benito looks down, and his hands shake. He starts crying. Then Manuel starts crying and they hug hard. The blood is all over both their faces, necks, and chests. One of them keeps saying, "Forgive me, forgive me," but it's hard to tell if it's Benito or Manuel.

Big Rafa gets up and stands above the hugging Tigres. He puts one big mitt on each boy's shoulder and separates them. Big Rafa barks at Manuel.

"Open your mouth, idiota." Manuel opens his mouth. Rafa looks disgusted.

"Spit it out so I can see in there," orders Rafa. Manuel spits out a bunch of blood. Rafa looks into his mouth again.

"This is bad," says Big Rafa. You cut right through your tongue. You need to go to the emergency room at Linda Hawkins Memorial now."

"It's only a cut," says Manuel. "I don't wanna go."

"NO," says my pa. "You're going to the hospital before I kick your ass some more for being so stupid."

"But—" Before Manuel can say what he wants to say, Pa points at him, and his finger is scary like a spear.

"Okay," says Manuel.

From the darkness outside of the tractor barn, I hear my ma's voice.

"Gordo!" she says. "Gordo!" I turn toward her voice, but I can't see her. She's like a ghost.

"Come here, hijo," she says.

"But Manuel's bleeding," I say.

"We're taking him to the hospital," says Big Rafa. "Go with your mom. Nobody worry." I walk toward Mom's voice. She puts her hand on my shoulder, and we begin walking toward our house.

"I'm sorry," she says.

"Why?" I ask.

"I should never let you stay with them when they're drinking. It's too crazy."

"But I wanted to be with them."

"What is that smell on you?" asks Ma.

"Nothing," I say. "They spilled some tequila on me."

"Never again," she says.

We get to the house and she goes in.

"Ma," I ask. "Can I sit on the front steps? I wanna see when they leave. I promise I'll stay right here." She looks at me real tired.

"Five minutes," she says. "Don't go anywhere. Then you come in."

Big Rafa brings his pickup and backs it up to the tractor barn. I hear them arguing about how to get Manuel to the hospital.

"Lay him down in the truck bed."

"No pendejo, he could choke on his own blood."

"Then put him on his side."

"He's hurt man, you can't lay him on a steel floor. He'll get more hurt."

"Sit him in the front with Rafa."

"No," says Big Rafa. "I'm not gonna get my seats and dash full of this idiot's blood. He rides in the bed." Finally Dad talks.

"Everybody listen. Here's the plan. We put my chair in the truck bed right against the cab. We sit Manuel down in the chair. Benito and Chulis, you sit on the floor next to him and watch that he doesn't fall off the chair. Cuatro, you help me lift my chair onto the truck." Pa and Cuatro try to lift the chair up, but they're too drunk. Cuatro is all wobbly in the knees, and Dad can barely walk straight. Then poor Cuatro, who's a tiny guy, drops his side of the chair and it falls on him, then Dad falls onto the chair. It's like a cartoon, and I want to laugh, but I don't. This is bad.

"Goddammit, Cuatro!" says Pa. He is smoking mad now, and everybody looks at him to see what happens next. He gets up. Juan Diego helps Pa stand his chair back up. Pa looks down at Cuatro, who is still on the ground, rubbing his leg. Dad and Juan Diego hold out their hands, and Cuatro takes them. They pull up little Cuatro like he's nothing.

"Sorry, Cuatro," says my pa. "You okay?"

"Yeah," says Cuatro. My pa turns to the guys.

"Muchachos, help us get the chair up into the truck bed." This time, four of them do it together, each one on a corner. They lift the green chair, drop it in the truck bed, and slide it till it bumps up against the cab. Dad looks over at Manuel, still bleeding at the mouth.

"Can you get up in the truck bed?" Manuel nods his head. He goes to climb up on the truck bed and almost falls back, but Juan Diego is right behind him and pushes him in. Manuel lands hard on his knees.

"Now Benito and Chulis help Manuel stand up and get into the chair," says my pa.

"No," says Manuel. He can barely talk, but he doesn't want any more help. He crawls to the chair on his hands and knees like a bleeding saint. He lifts himself up and sits down real slow, like an old man. Benito goes next to the chair on one side and gets down on one knee. He puts one hand on the chair and one on Manuel's shoulder. Chulis does the same on the other side. Dad shuts the gate on the truck bed, climbs into the front seat with Rafa, and closes the door. The truck begins moving. Big Rafa is drunk, but he goes down the bumpy dirt road really slow. Juan Diego waves and waves goodbye.

The truck crawls toward San Juan Highway to get to the hospital. Manuel, sitting up in the truck bed, is like a bloody prince on a green throne. Benito and Chulis are the servants protecting him and holding him up, like he's special. The red taillights on the back of the truck slowly get smaller and smaller. I feel like Doctor Strange in a comic book, flying outside of my body and watching a sad float in a night parade that no one else wants to see.

Alex

It's Saturday morning and my pa isn't drunk today. He wasn't drunk last night either, so I feel pretty lucky, and my ma does too. When I wake up, she's in the kitchen playing her album of Los Panchos. It's nice to hear her singing again. Ma has been kind of sad since we moved out of San Juan Bautista and came to Watsonville about five months ago. We have our own house now, and it's nicer. We have a flush toilet, a lawn, and a telephone. We moved because my pa got a job at Hirano Chicken Ranch near Watsonville. Ma got a new job too, at the Jolly Giant vegetable plant. They don't have to work in the sun anymore, so that's good, but I miss the Gyrich Farms Worker Camp. I miss living next door to my nana and grandpa. I don't have friends at my new school, Las Lomas Elementary. Not yet. Maybe next year I can have a friend.

I stay in bed and listen to Ma in the kitchen. Even before she calls everyone to come and eat, I smell her fresh flour tortillas and coffee. When the house smells like that, it feels like maybe we're doing okay. She calls us, and we go to eat. Even my big sister, Sylvie, the seventh-grade, full-time professional snot, looks pretty happy at the table.

I serve myself beans and fried eggs and sit down at the table. I'm rolling up a hot tortilla to take my first bite when we suddenly hear a weird little motor noise from next door. It sounds like a pissed-off baby lawn mower. Everyone looks out the window to our neighbor Alex's place to see what it is. At first, nobody sees nothing, and then I look up and see him. Alex is waaaay up in his acacia tree. He has his legs wrapped around a branch and he's holding a buzzing chain saw. He has a blue bandana wrapped around his head like a cholo, even though he's not a gangster. He's too old for that, maybe forty or more. His work shirtsleeves are rolled up to the elbows, and he has on brown leather gloves.

Last week, the rain and wind were wild. They knocked a huge branch off Alex's acacia tree, and it crashed into the little chicken coop he made and killed two of his little red chickens. I heard he made caldo de pollo out of them, so they didn't die for nothing, but now I guess he wants to cut off some tree branches before another storm happens and another branch falls and maybe kills him or his mean junkyard dog, Choco.

"Alex es un diablo," says my ma. "Climbs like a monkey. Look how he got way up in that tree with that big saw."

"Pfft," says my pa. "No safety rope. That idiota is gonna fall."

Soon as he says that, the branch breaks, and Alex falls. It's like my pa did a magic trick. Alex drops behind the rusted and busted cyclone fence covered with ivy between our yards. I hear the chain saw cough one time, then it don't say nothin'.

I stand up first, then everybody does the same. We look at each other, and nobody knows what to do for a second, then BOOM! Sylvie goes flying out the back door. I book on out right behind her, slamming the screen door against the wall on my way out. We run up Hudson Street to get to Alex's. Ma and Pa are walking fast behind us. We sprint up Alex's driveway, through the side gate, and into his backyard. Sylvie's fast and arrives first. I'm right behind her. Alex's big black-and-tan dog, Choco, is barking like crazy, standing on his back legs, pulling on his heavy chain. He's as tall as me and you can see his big cojones swinging and jumping around when he pulls on the chain and tries to get closer to Alex.

There's all this blood on Alex's side. He's on his back with his eyes closed up tight and making awful noises that sound like laughing but it's not laughing and sounds like a woman but it's not no woman. It's Alex. His legs are halfway covered in the leaves and yellow flowers of the broken acacia branch. His chain saw is way over by the trash cans. Three chickens have flown up to the roof of the chicken coop and they're looking at the action like they're in a stadium watching El Puma wrestling against Diabolico for the championship belt. Alex is really jacked up. His arm don't look right. It has a weird bend, like when you take the arm off a Barbie and pop it back in backward. Also, it looks like some bone or something is trying to pop out from under the skin.

I get on my knees next to Alex, but I don't know what to do.

"Are you okay, Alex?"

"No, Gordo. I'm not okay," says Alex. Behind me, my ma and pa arrive. My pa whispers, "Chingue su madre" and gets down on his knees next to me. Alex's eyes are closing and his head is dropping to the side. Pa calls Alex's name.

"Alex, Alex. Look at me. Que te pasa?" asks Pa. Alex can't answer. He keeps saying, "Ay ay ay." Ma has her hand over her mouth, and she's shaking her head like she's saying no, then she turns to Sylvie.

"Sylvie, run to the house and call the operator, and tell them to send a, what do you call them? Chingado . . . it's the hospital vans, the white ones with the whoo whoo!"

"The ambulance?" says Sylvie.

"Yes, the ambulancia. Call them right now! Go, muchacha!" Sylvie runs off and now Alex is quiet and closing his eyes, like he's gonna fall asleep. Pa is slapping Alex on the cheeks, telling him to wake up. Alex opens his eyes. He looks around like he doesn't know where he is.

"What happened?" asks Alex.

"You had a bad fall, Alex. You're probably confused. It's me," says Pa, "your neighbor Antonio. Do you understand what happened?"

"Yes. No. Yes. I fell."

"That's right. You fell out of the tree. We calling the ambulance." Alex tries to move, and it hurts him. He groans again.

"Don't worry, Alex," says Ma. "They'll be here in a minute. We'll stay here with you till they arrive, okay?" With his good arm, Alex tries to pull down his sweatshirt zipper.

"Alex, don't try to move—you have a big cut on your side. Let me look," says Ma. Ma kneels in the dirt and unzips the bloody sweatshirt and opens it. Oh God. It's like he got machine-gunned. So much red. Through the tear in his shirt, you can see a long cut that looks like a giant mouth with bloody lips.

"Ai, Dios mio," says Ma when she sees this.

"Viejo, give me your shirt," says my ma. Pa takes off his shirt. Ma rolls it up like a burrito and presses it on Alex's side. Alex makes terrible noises. Choco is barking and snarling and looking right at me like it's all my damned fault.

The Hudson Street dogs hear the ambulance first, and they start howling, first King up the hill, then Nelly, Pepita, Apache, Boomer, and even old Red. It's like a chorus, and Choco starts howling too. Soon I can hear the ambulance coming up the road and stopping in front of Alex's house. The ambulance guys get out. They kind of look like Officers Jon and Poncherello from the TV show *CHiPs*! *CHiPs* is the best television show ever in all of 1977 and me and all the other fifth graders at Las Lomas Elementary love the motorcycle police on *CHiPs*! The gringo officer Jon is tall with blond feathered hair and a mustache. The other one's Mexican, and he looks a little like Elvis when he was skinny. His hair is combed back and super black like Superman's. Officer Poncherello sees the blood everywhere, and he stays calm. He starts to ask Alex some questions.

"Can you wiggle your fingers?" Alex does.

"Can you lift your head?" Alex tries. He screams. No good.

Officer Jon bends over a black case with a zipper, and his perfect golden feathers fall across his forehead. He pulls out these long scissors with roundy tips.

"Okay, my friend, what is your name?" says Officer Jon.

"Alex."

"Alex, my friend, we need to get a look at your arm and your side. We need to cut off your sweatshirt and T-shirt because we can't take them off without hurting you, okay?"

"No," says Alex. Alex looks scared. Maybe Officer Jon's English is too fast for Alex to understand.

"Can you tell him in Spanish?" I ask them. Officer Poncherello explains it in Spanish, and then Alex says no again.

"Alex, this is an emergency, una emergencia," says Poncherello. "You're really hurt and we need to cut these off so we can help you. Is that okay?" Alex is quiet for a moment, like he's thinking about it. Why is he thinking about it?

"Okay, yes," says Alex.

* * *

The gringo begins cutting off Alex's sweatshirt up the side and folding it open like a newspaper he is about to read. Then he cuts into a black T-shirt. Then a dark green T-shirt. Then a bloody white tank top. Jesus, how many shirts is Alex wearing? Under the tank top, I see that Alex is already wearing a bandage on his chest. What??? The ambulance guys look at each other. They're confused too. The bandage is full of blood on one side, and I see something coming out from underneath the bandage—oh my God.

A GIANT BOOB.

I know fat dudes have boobs. When we fight, Sylvie always tells me I have big boobs, and I'm not normal. But that boob is big, like a woman's.

"Gordo," says Pa. "You and Sylvie go home."

"But I wanna see," I say.

"GO!" says Pa. I look at him, and he is giving me his hard look. I know that look. It's time to go home. Me and Sylvie walk away. As soon as we get far enough, we begin to talk.

"Did you see that?" I ask Sylvie.

"Of course I saw those big tetas. I was right there too, dummy."

"Man, oh man," I say. "I never seen a man with such big chichis."

"What are you talking about?" asks Sylvie.

"I'm talking about Alex, dumbass," I say to her. "Alex has big boobs for a man."

"Jesus Christ," says Sylvie. "I can't believe you're so dumb. Alex is not a man, bozo."

"What?" I say. "What do you mean?"

"Alex is not a man. He's a woman. She's a woman. Didn't you know?"

"But Alex dresses like a man. He fixes the car, does all the man stuff. Even his voice, he sounds like a man. Mostly."

"But he's not. She's a woman." She starts laughing at me.

"Why are you laughing?"

"I can't believe you, Gordo," she says. "I can't believe you are such a moron, who doesn't know who's a man and who's a woman."

"How was I supposed to know, Sylvie?" I say. "No one told me." She's laughing so hard she can hardly talk. Sylvie laughs as we go up our driveway and back into the house. She sits in her spot at the kitchen table and shakes her head like she can't believe what she's seeing.

"I don't understand," I say. "Does Alex have a wiener or does he got a pussy?"

"Of course, you can't have big ol' boobs and a wiener at the same time. She has a pussy. She's a woman dressed up like a man. That's all."

"Why? Why does Alex dress up like a man if he's not?"

"Because that's what she wants to do. Instead of being a normal lady, she wants to look like some old guy with a crappy mustache."

"Dang, Sylvie. That's cold-blooded. Alex never did nothing to you. He's just different," I say.

"Different is the same thing as creepy. Look at her. And think about it. Have you ever seen anyone visiting her since we moved here? Have you ever seen a sister visit her?"

"No."

"A brother? A cousin? A tia?"

"No."

"A friend. You ever see a friend visit?"

"No, I guess not."

"Why do you think no one visits?"

"Maybe he likes to be alone."

"Naw, bozo. She's a creepy weirdo. Only that evil dog, Choco, likes her."

"Alex is just different, Sylvie. Everybody is different."

"She's too different."

I don't know what to say no more, so I shut up. I guess Alex really is too different and creepy, now that Sylvie said that. Sometimes I feel different too. Maybe I'm creepy like Alex. Sylvie and a bunch of boys at school, they're always telling me I'm a sissy. Everything I do is a problem: the way I laugh, throw a baseball, or run. They tell me I talk like a big, fat girl. I tell them "shut up" or "fuck you" and mostly "leave me alone." Sometimes they do leave me alone, sometimes they don't. It's not a good idea to be different.

We both look out the window to see the action at Alex's. Jon and Poncherello roll the wheely bed down the driveway to the ambulance. Alex is lying in the bed and his bloody arm and good leg are wrapped in bandages. They open the back doors of the ambulance, fold up the wheels, and roll in the wheely bed. They drive off with the sirens on, and the dog chorus says goodbye to poor Alex.

My ma and pa come back to our kitchen and sit at the table. The food is cold, but we all start eating. Everybody's talking about every little thing that happened at Alex's, but nobody is talking about the boobs. I feel like I'm gonna go crazy if somebody doesn't talk about the boobs.

"I thought Alex was a man," I finally say. Sylvie laughs at me. She talks to me, but she doesn't make any sounds. I watch her mouth, and I can see she is saying "stuuuuupid."

"I thought you knew," says my ma.

"So all this time you knew?" I ask.

"Of course I knew, hijo."

"Then why didn't you tell me?"

"Because you never asked. Didn't you notice, couldn't you see, hijo?"

"But you always talked about him like he was a man."

"He is like a man," says Ma.

"But Ma—" I start to say.

"Basta. That's enough of that," says Pa. "We're gonna eat this nice machaca, drink our coffee, and we're not gonna talk about that marimacha anymore, okay?"

"Okay, okay," I say. "But what's a marimacha?" Pa gives me the look again.

"Never mind," I say. Pa is eating angry. I can see the muscles in his neck moving.

Two days later, I'm helping my pa hang a new screen door when we see a yellow taxicab pull up into Alex's driveway. I have never seen a yellow taxi in real life, only in the movies. The back door opens, and I see Alex. He gets out of the car real slow. He has one arm in a cast and in the other he has a big paper bag with handles. He—she—begins to walk, bent over like a beat-up old hunchback. My pa stops working and raises his hand at Alex like an Indian chief. Alex sees him. She looks like she wishes she hadn't seen him. Alex moves his head a little toward my pa and waves a little at me. I wave back. He opens the door, walks in, and closes it behind him.

Later that day, my ma makes chicken enchiladas and lines up six hot ones on a plate and covers them with 'luminim foil. She tells me to take it over to Alex. I don't want to go to Alex's house. Seems like he's a different person now that she's really a woman. I walk the enchiladas over to Alex's and knock on the door. Choco hears me and starts barking. While I wait for Alex to get the door, I start to feel a little nervous. Sylvie is right. Alex is sort of creepy, if you think about it. I don't want to be here at her house.

Alex opens the door. Hair all wild, striped pajamas, no shoes. She has dark circles around her eyes, like she lost a mean fight.

"Hi," I say. "My ma sent this to you." I hold out the plate in front of me. "Chicken enchiladas."

"Thank you, Gordo," says Alex. She takes the plate. "Tell your mami I love chicken enchiladas and God bless her."

"Okay, I'll tell her you said thanks." Alex smiles. I never seen her smile before.

She puts down the plate on a little cabinet by the door. She waves goodbye with her good hand. I wave goodbye, and Alex closes the door. Maybe Alex isn't a creep, just a little weird.

A few days later, my pa is mowing the lawn and I'm raking, and Alex limps up Hudson Street to our driveway. In one hand, she has a cane, in the other, a bag. She is limping but looks better. Her hair is combed, her clothes is clean.

"Hola, Antonio," she says to my pa.

"Alex," he says. "How are you doing? You're looking strong like Tarzan." They laugh.

"I'm doing better. I have something for you," says Alex, "to thank you for helping me when I fell."

"You don't have to give us anything. We're glad to help."

"No, no," says Alex. "You were all helpful. You even took care of Choco while I was away. I saw that he had food and water when I came home. I want to give you this." She gives Pa the bag. He takes it, reaches in, and pulls out a beautiful bottle. It's long and round on the bottom, kind of like the genie bottle in the TV show *I Dream of Jeannie*, except it's blue. The cap is a giant blue diamond. My pa looks surprised.

"Caramba. Tequila El Máximo?" says Pa. "This fine tequila is too much."

"I brought back two bottles last time I went to Jalisco. I got them for a special day. I want you to have it. Please."

"Thank you. I've never had it," says my pa. Alex smiles a crooked smile.

"I have glasses," says Alex. She pulls out two tiny glasses from her pants pocket. Pa smiles. I don't know if Pa likes Alex, but I know he loves tequila. And beer. Plus whiskey. He grabs the big diamond bottle top and opens it. He holds the bottle up to his nose, closes his eyes, and smells it. He smiles, like he's smelling cookies in the oven or something.

"This smells really good," he says to Alex.

"The label says El Máximo, so we'll see about that," says Alex. Pa takes a tiny glass from Alex, and he pours out a drink for each of them. Alex holds his glass up, and they clink their glasses together.

"Salud," says Alex.

"Salud," says Pa. Pa drinks one small gulp. Alex drinks it all in a second. Pa looks happy.

"This is nice, Alex, but I feel bad accepting such fine tequila."

"I live alone, Antonio. If you and Señora Esperanza hadn't helped me, I could have passed out and bled to death, who knows. I owe you."

"You should have someone move in with you," says my pa. "Think about it. You're a woman, and women shouldn't live alone. Too dangerous."

"Maybe so, maybe so," says Alex. "I have to go now. I never thanked your mujer for the enchiladas. They were so good."

"I'll let her know," says Pa. Alex waves at me and walks away. I wave goodbye. Pa looks at the bottle and whistles.

"So nice," he says. He looks at Alex like he is confused. "So strange."

About two weeks later, I'm riding my bicycle up the street, and Alex comes around the corner in her beat-up red truck, and there is a pretty girl riding with her. I remember what Sylvie said about Alex never having visitors, so of course I feel nosy, and I have to check it out. I stop along the side of the road and wave at them so they'll look at me and I can get a better look. They pull into the driveway and they both step out. The girl smiles at me. She's super pretty. It's like a movie star landed here on Hudson Street. Beautiful round face, light skin, big brown eyes, nice smile, pretty dress with flowers.

Alex goes to the back of her Toyota pickup and opens up the tailgate. There are two suitcases and a bunch of cardboard boxes tied up with rope. She uses her good hand to try to unload the truck bed, but she's having a hard time moving the boxes around with only one hand.

"You want me to help you with the bags?" I ask.

"No thanks, Gordo," says Alex. "We've got them." She turns to the pretty girl, saying, "This is Delia. She's going to live here from now on."

"Hola, I'm Delia," she says. We shake hands.

"I'm Gordo. I live over there," I say, pointing to the house.

"Good to meet you," she says. "Your house is pretty."

"Thank you," I say. I get embarrassed. Our house isn't pretty. It's tiny, and it's pink with blue, like a stupid baby shower. I hate pink, but every other Mexican loves pink because that's the color they always use to paint houses. Still, Delia is pretty, so if she thinks the house is pretty, maybe it is, and I never noticed.

"Nice to meet you," I say to Delia. "I'll see you later." I head up the street to finish my ride. I look back at her as I ride away. Her hair is really long and shiny. Delia is like the collie dog Lassie. Everything about her is pretty.

As I ride my bike up Hudson Street, I think that if Alex is like a guy, maybe Delia is like her girlfriend. They're like jotos, but they're both girls, and one is not girly. If they really are girlfriends, Alex got lucky, because Delia is foxy and nice.

For a while, we don't hear anything more about Delia. Everything is quiet at their house, except for Alex coming and going to work at Coast Mushrooms. Then one morning, while my pa is at work, Alex visits us at our house with Delia. We have never had Alex in our house, but my ma is very cool about it. She loves visitors.

"Come in, come in," says my ma. I want to sit with them at the kitchen table and listen to their stories, but I know Ma is gonna chase me away if I do because that talk is not for kids. Instead of trying to stay in the kitchen, I go to the living room and sit on the sofa closest to the kitchen and pretend to read *Encyclopedia Brown Gets His Man*.

Of course, Ma asks them if they're hungry.

"No, no, we already had breakfast."

"Coffee?"

"Yes, coffee would be nice," says Alex.

"Now that I'm settling in next door, I really wanted to meet you, Señora Esperanza," says Delia.

When Alex introduces Ma, it's the most royal introduction.

"Esperanza is a good woman. A great mother," says Alex. "The best neighbor possible. A magnificent woman." Ma looks embarrassed and laughs a little.

"So how has it been so far, Delia?" asks Ma.

"It's different here. It's kind of cold. All that fog in the mornings. When I ride to town with Alex and it's foggy at night, I feel like I'm in a monster movie." Everyone laughs.

"The hometown," asks Ma, "is it very warm?"

"Yes," says Delia. "Tropical."

"Don't worry about the fog," says Ma. "You'll get used to it. So tell me, what are your plans now that you're here in Watsonville?"

"I've been working at the mushrooms," says Delia.

"Coast Mushrooms. With me," says Alex.

"I work and send back money to my madre. I want to keep working, earn money, send more money back home. I want her to use the money to send my younger sister to high school so she can be a secretary or a bank teller. Educated. Not like me."

"Delia and I first met at the mushroom plant," says Alex.

"Alex is a manager there," says Delia.

"Not a manager," says Alex. "I'm only a shift supervisor."

"She tells everyone what to do, even the men," says Delia. "If I do a good job there, maybe I'll be a manager one day too. I'll tell those hairy men what to do." Delia and Ma laugh, then Alex talks.

"Delia thinks it's a good idea to keep working at the mushroom plant. At first, I agreed, but now I think that's a bad idea. The women are all gossips and traitors, and the men are pigs. It's not safe for you there, Delia. You should stay home."

"But I need to work and make money," says Delia.

"That's not a good idea," says Alex. "I think you need to stay home and not be out there running around. This is not El Salvador. You don't know how things work around here."

"But I need to work and help my family and pay for my expenses. I like working."

"I'm paying for the food, the rent. You don't have to worry, Chiquita."

"But—"

"And I can give you money for your family," says Alex. "This discussion is boring our host, Esperanza, so we're not going to talk about this here anymore."

"If Delia is not going to be working at the mushroom plant, maybe she can take some English classes," says my ma.

"That's a good idea," says Delia.

"Absolutely," says my ma. "In this country, if you want to succeed, you have to learn English. I learned a little. The basics. They give free classes at the library. We can go there to sign you up. You'll need to fill out some papers, but Gordo or Sylvie can help you. They're good at doing papers. They do them all the time for me and Antonio."

"Gracias. Que bonito," says Delia. "Your kids have two languages. They can help you."

"When they first started kindergarten, they only spoke Spanish. But the little ones, they're like sponges. They learn it like it's nothing. Tell me about your country, Delia. What part of Mexico is El Salvador in? Is it pretty?" asks Ma. Delia is quiet. Alex is quiet.

"It's a different country from Mexico. It's very pretty," says Delia. "The country is very green, big trees, like a jungle. So many greens, you can't imagine. We have lakes, volcanoes. I don't mean to brag, but my country is beautiful. And sad. And dangerous. You can't imagine."

"Why is that?" asks Ma.

"The government, Doña. No one is safe. My two brothers, they were in San Salvador protesting the elections. They said the elections were stolen, and the government murdered them."

"Oh no," says Ma. I stop breathing. When Delia speaks again, she sounds like she wants to cry.

"We think they got killed, but we don't know for sure because they got disappeared. We never even got to see their bodies. My beautiful brothers. They say the government shot the protesters and even innocent people walking by."

"Ave Maria purisima, how terrible," whispers my ma. I lean toward the kitchen to hear better.

"My mother and father and me, we went to the hospitals, to the police offices, and finally to the army offices to ask for the bodies. We filled out all these papers at the office and waited almost five hours. Then they came back and told us that nobody died, that there was no massacre. It was just the police trying to control a violent gang and now the criminals are in jail. They told us to go to look for my violent gang brothers in jail. I told them my brothers weren't criminals. They were just protesting. Then that soldier looked me right in the eyes and said, 'What you're saying about people getting killed are lies against the government, señorita. If you or your family ever come back and say such things, we'll throw you all in jail for anti-government defamation. Or worse.' He put his hand on my shoulder and squeezed hard and said, 'You should be careful. A girl should be careful, because there are dangerous people out there who do bad things. We have your address now, and we will come by if we learn anything. I hope your family is not involved in any violence in the future. We know where you live, señorita. Are there others like you? Maybe some sisters?'"

"Dios santo," says Ma.

"I felt my heart drop down to my feet when the army officer said that. Because everybody has heard the story of girls, sometimes only thirteen years old, getting kidnapped and . . ." I hear a spoon stirring coffee in a cup. I hear a goat in the field up the hill. She doesn't say nothing more, so you know it must be something really bad. "Then we started seeing cars with suspicious men parked on the street near our house. It was so frightening."

"So you had to run away," says my ma. "Ay, Delia. How terrible. Do you have family nearby?"

"No. Not in California. No one came with me," says Delia. "It's bad back home, but they didn't want to leave. Almost my entire family is back there. The grandparents. The uncles and aunts, the cousins. We have little businesses. A corner store. A guava orchard. My uncle fixes cars. They didn't want to leave that behind. My mother said she wanted to live and die in her own country." I hear somebody sigh, but I don't know who it is. Then I hear someone crying.

"It's okay, Chiquita, it's okay. Don't cry," Alex is saying.

"This is so sad," my ma replies. "No family near you. You had to escape all by yourself. Nobody should be without a family to help them."

"Esperanza, I'm sorry," says Delia. "I've known you for five minutes and already I'm telling you all these terrible things."

"It's okay, Delia. Tell your story or it'll drown you. And I'm glad you escaped, but how did you do it?" asks Ma.

"My mother and father pulled together the money. My uncle drove me across the border to Guatemala City. From there I took buses across the border into Mexico, all the way to Tijuana. I got robbed on the bus by a man with a knife the second night. But I was ready. I gave him some money, cried like a baby for show, but most of my money was in a secret pocket my tia had sewn inside of my blouse. The next day, I met a family on the bus, and we pretended I was part of the family so people wouldn't know I was traveling alone. When I got to Tijuana, I walked up to the border and asked the border guard for asylum. They filled out my papers and told me it would take three or four weeks. I started crying, because I didn't know what I'd do by myself for a month.

"The border office lady told me I could stay at the Sweet Name of Mary church in Tijuana. 'Walk toward the tall spire with the cross,' she said. I did and arrived at the church. Father Ignacio and the sisters were saints. I stayed for almost three weeks, along with other families trying to get asylum.

"Before I left, Sister Sarita connected me with the Roques, a host family that was ready to take in someone like me. I got to talk to them on the phone. They were Salvadoreans too. When I got permission to cross to the United States, Sister Sarita walked me across the border and put me on a bus to Salinas. She even gave me fifty-five dollars. Imagine that. The church was so poor, so many people to help, and she gave me money. Saints. I got on the bus and in one day, I arrived. The Roque family was a good family, even though the wife was a Jehovah's Witness."

"You go through all that suffering and then end up with Jehovah's Witnesses?"

"They're just like anyone else," says Delia.

"No they're not," says my ma. "They don't like Catholicism and want to bring down our church. Did she try to convert you?"

"From the first day, she tried to convert me. Can you imagine? Saint Christopher and the Virgin guide me to California without a scratch, and she wants me to change religion? No thank you, señora. I like my faith. Besides, their mass takes half a day."

"Eternities," says my ma. "You feel like a soul trapped in purgatory. Terrible." Everyone in the kitchen starts laughing. I cover my mouth with my fist and laugh too.

"So how did you meet Alex?" asks my ma.

"The host family helped me get a job at the mushroom plant, thank the Lord," says Delia. "That's where I met Alex, and we became friends. Very good friends. Now here we are. Starting a new life."

"A new start together," says Alex.

"I'm glad for you, muchacha," says Ma. "You're a good person, I can tell. So young, so pretty, and you've gone through all this. But God is great, and now you're here on Hudson Street. You're safe. You can have a better life and help your family over there."

"That's what matters," says Delia.

"We all matter," says Alex. "They matter. I matter too. Just like your family."

"Señora Esperanza," says Delia. "I kept hearing such nice things about you, and I see now that all the nice things Alejandra said about you were true."

Alejandra. Alex's real name is Alejandra.

"Señora," says Delia. "I want to ask a favor. When I need advice, can I come to you?"

"No, Delia," says Alex before Ma can answer. "Don't bother Señora Esperanza. She is very busy with her family and working."

"You can always come to me for help, Delia," says Ma.

"Thank you," says Delia.

"We'll see," says Alex. "Oh, look at the time. Thank you for the coffee. We should get going now, señora." I hear them pushing back their chairs as they leave the table. I walk into the kitchen to wave goodbye. Delia waves goodbye at us and says thank you three times before they go out the door.

They killed her brothers. She had to run away from home. Someone robbed her. Some people have to walk around with so many sad stories. They have to get up, brush their teeth, wash their face, go to work like everybody else, but they're not like everyone else.

For days, I think about the things Alex and Delia said, and I decide that Alex is not a creepy weirdo. She dresses up like a guy, but she helped Delia escape. She's one of the good guys.

Sometimes on Sundays, I see Delia and Alex get all dressed up to go to church. Alex wears a guayabera shirt with a sharp crease down the front, khakis, and a nice hat with a little red feather in it. To tell the truth, Alex is not very pretty. But ever since Delia arrived, Alex looks good on Sundays. I never seen her dressed up so nice. One Sunday, she wore a blue guayabera shirt with matching shoes the color of a bluebird egg. For church, Delia always wears a dress down to her knees and lets her hair down.

If you saw them all dressed in Easter colors on a Sunday, you'd probably think they look pretty happy. But I know they're not, because sometimes I hear the bad sounds coming from their house. I know the bad sounds from when Pa returns home drunk and angry. From Alex's house, I hear shouting. Things breaking. Scared screams. Somebody making noises like an angry animal. I once heard Delia begging Alex not to hit her, but of course she didn't stop. It never works when you ask someone to stop hitting you.

A few weeks later, I'm hanging clothes on the clothesline, and I hear my name. It's soft at first, so I don't really notice it, but it gets louder.

"gordo."

"Gordo."

"GORDO."

I can't figure out where the voice is coming from, till I notice it's coming from the ivy fence between our house and Alex's.

"It's me, Delia," says the ivy.

"Hi Delia," I say. "I didn't see you."

"Gordo, I'm wondering, do you know how to fix this?" I hear the sounds of ivy leaves and vines getting pushed aside. Then I see Delia's hand holding a transistor radio with a suitcase handle on top. She pushes it through a hole in the fence over to our side. I walk toward the hand and take the radio.

"Your radio is broken?" I ask.

"Yes. No. I don't know. Maybe." I take the radio from her hand.

"Turn it on," says Delia. I find the on/off button and push it. The radio starts playing "When I Need You." I change the station and it's Cornelio Reyna's "Barrio Pobre." I change it again and it's a football game. Boring. I change it one more time and it's "Rock the Boat." That's my song! I turn up the volume, and it sounds good.

"Your radio sounds okay to me, Delia."

"I know the sound is good, but it's broken. It's different. I brought this radio from El Salvador. I wanted to know what was happening back in my country, but when I turn it on here, it mostly talks in English. I can't hear the radio voices from home. I turn the dial to where the news should be, and all I hear is rock and roll in English. What happened to the voices from home?"

I'm not sure how to explain it, but I try.

"The radio, it's different in every place," I say. "When we go visit family in San Jose, the radio is different. Different music, different news. You can't hear the voices from back home in your country. They're too far away."

"Oh," says Delia. I can tell from her "oh" that this is sad news.

"I really wanted to hear the voices from home," says Delia. "I miss them so much. It makes me feel lonely. I thought the voices from home lived inside the radio, and I could bring them to Watsonville."

"You can't."

"I'm so stupid," she says. "I'm a burra."

"No you're not, Delia. You just didn't know how the radio works. Here, let me give you back your radio." Delia pushes back some ivy like a curtain on her end. Through the hole, I see a corner of her face. She has a puffy eye. It is black with purple. I don't say nothing. I push the radio through the ivy, and she takes it.

"Thanks, Gordo," she says. She sounds so sad.

I hear her walking away. I hear her back door open and then shut. I finish hanging the clothes. I'm not sure what to do. Ma is always telling me to mind my own business. Says I'm like some nosy old lady. Black eyes are top secret. Two times Ma got a black eye from Pa, and nobody said nothing about it. I guess you're supposed to shut up like nothing happened and swallow the story. But Delia needs help, so what should I do? I look up at the sky, close my eyes, and I ask God to tell me what to do. I wait and wait, hanging clothes, and he don't say nothing. Every time I ask for help, he never says nothing. I finish hanging the clothes and go back into the house. Sylvie is doing homework at the kitchen table. Ma is cleaning the living room windows. I open my sock drawer and grab my Magic 8-Ball. I know it's stupid to ask a toy what to do, but I'm stuck. I hold the black ball close to my mouth and I whisper, "Should I tell Ma about Delia's black eye?"

I shake the ball and stare at the little round window with the blue water. My answer floats up to the window.

"ASK AGAIN LATER." Stupid ball. I shake the ball hard and ask again. "SIGNS POINT TO YES," says the ball. Okay, that's it. I've decided. I'm gonna tell.

When I tell her, my ma looks worried and asks me to show her where I talked to Delia through the fence. We go there, and Ma begins calling out to Delia. At first, we don't hear nothing from Delia's place. She probably can't hear Ma. But Choco starts barking at us. Ma calls her name again. Finally, we hear Delia's back door open.

"Delia, is that you?" says Ma.

"Hola, Esperanza," says Delia.

"Hola, hija," says Ma. "Come have a little coffee with me?"

"Thanks. But I can't go right now," says Delia.

"Can you visit later?" says Ma.

"I can't."

"Just for a few minutes, please visit for coffee. I want to see you." Delia is quiet for a moment.

"I can't," she says again. She sounds like she wants to cry. "I want to visit, but my front fence is locked. Alex locks me in when she leaves for work in the morning. Wraps the chain around the front gate and locks it. She wears the key around her neck."

"Dios mio," says Ma. "What's happening here? What if there's an emergency and you need to leave? What if firemen need to get in?"

"She's getting so jealous," Delia says. "We go to church, we go to the groceries, and she comes back mad, accusing me of making eyes at men and trying to get them to look at me."

"Oh my God," says Ma. "You're like a prisoner, Delia."

"I don't know what to do," says Delia.

"I want to see your face," asks Ma.

"Okay," says Delia.

Ma pushes her hands into the ivy and spreads it open. Delia does the same thing on the other side. I see Ma pressing her lips together and her face is red.

"She did this to you?" asks Ma. "Cabrona."

"I don't know what to do," says Delia. Ma puts her face right up to the hole in the ivy. "Don't cry, hija. You have to listen to me. You have to fight back. Nobody likes to fight, but you have to fight back. Scratch. Bite. Kick. Throw things. Fight like an animal. Make her pay every time she tries to hit you. That's what I had to do with Antonio. It makes them angry at first, and sometimes they get even more violent, but sometimes they learn, and then they think twice. Antonio stopped it eventually. I was scared, but I kept fighting back. You fight back too."

"I'm afraid, Esperanza."

"Of course you are. But Delia, think of how brave you are. You escaped your country, and you got here. All by yourself. Tell me something. Did your father hit you when you were growing up?" asks my ma.

"He could be mean. He never hit us."

"Think about that. Your own father never hit you, and now you're going to let Alex hit you? Alex isn't even blood to you. Why should she get to hit you?"

"I don't know. She gets so angry," says Delia.

"Then you get angry too. Fight back. Make her pay. Every time. It's the only thing they understand. My god. Alex is just like a man."

"Worse," says Delia. "I had two boyfriends before Alex, and they never hit me."

"That is because they were still boyfriends, señorita. They were trying to win you. At first, it's all kisses and roses and velvet boxes with ugly earrings they pick out. As soon as you get married, POW! That sweet lover disappears and gets replaced by a husband, and let me tell you, things change." Delia laughs and Ma joins in.

"Oh they change all right. At first they don't even want to fart in front of you. They leave the room to fart. So delicate. Then later, they've got you, and they really don't care anymore, and they fire away. Like a machine gun. Help me, Saint Jude of the lost causes." They are laughing hard now. I pretend to rake, but look the other way so Ma doesn't see me laughing too.

"Ay, Esperanza," says Delia, "the things you say. I just realized I hadn't laughed in days. It feels so good."

Ma and Delia begin talking through the fence every day. Even when it rains, they're out there with their umbrellas, talking.

Delia says talking in person is safer, because Alex always checks the phone bill and makes Delia explain every call. A few weeks later, Alex hits Delia again. Of course I got as close as I could to listen when they talked.

"Why'd it happen?" asks Ma.

"I asked if I could start working again at the mushroom plant, and Alex asked if I had some secret lover I wanted to meet at the plant, and from there she got angrier and angrier, and I got angry too and told her she was crazy, and she slapped me and punched my face and stomach."

"Did you fight back?" Delia don't say nothing.

"I didn't fight back," says Delia. "But I told her afterward that I wanted to leave her."

"What did she say?"

"Alex got very calm. The quiet, it was scarier than shouting and hitting. She said I would never leave her. She says she helped me by letting me stay with her, and now I owe her my life, and I have to stay with her. She said she had ways of watching me, even when she isn't there. She told me she has an invisible eye that never sleeps. It follows me. I can't escape."

"She sounds crazy."

"Alex said the invisible eye will lead her to me, and she'll find me and drag me back home by the hair. She told me she has been slowly gathering everything she needs to destroy my life if I ever leave her. My hair from a hairbrush. My fingernail clippings. My underwear. My picture."

"You're saying Alex is a witch?" asks Ma.

"I never used to believe in that witch stuff," says Delia, "but now I don't know what to think. I only know I'm scared."

"If Alex is doing brujería against you, you need protection," says Ma. "I know a curandera. She is really good. Good prices too. I can bring her, and she can do works that will protect you."

"I don't know, señora. I can't understand Alex. Sometimes she really is sweet. Most of the time, she is normal. But then she gets angry, and it's like she gets possessed. Lately she has been saying she doesn't want to be alone, but if I don't do as she says, she is going to call the migra and tell them I've been selling drugs, and they will send me back to El Salvador. I told her she couldn't lie that way to the migra. She said the migra will always believe a citizen over an immigrant. Do you think it's true, about me being deported back to my country if she tells them that lie about the drugs?"

"No," says my ma. "It's probably not true. You're not illegal. You have the right papers, the permission to stay here. She's trying to scare you."

"I don't need a magic spell. I need to escape," says Delia. "I have a cousin. He moved to Chicago a few months ago. When I arrived in Watsonville, I sent him a letter telling him I was okay, and I gave him the phone number. He calls once in a while. Last time he called, I told him everything. He was mad and said he'd come and beat up Alex if I wanted him to, or he can send me a bus ticket to Chicago, and I could go there and live with him. He works in a big hotel, in the laundry room, and he says I could work there or cleaning rooms."

"Do it, Delia," says my ma. "Go."

"You're right. I have to go before something terrible happens."

"Something terrible happened already. She hits you. Locks you up. She's probably done brujería on you. What more do you want?"

"You're right. I tried to make it work with Alex. I loved Alex, but she killed that. I don't want any more of this. I'm going to accept the bus ticket to Chicago from my cousin. To escape, I need help getting my bags over the fence and to the bus station. Can you help me, Esperanza?"

"Yes," said Ma. "I'll get my brother Hector. He can help you get your things out and drive you to the bus station. When do you want to escape?"

"I don't know yet. I can give you my cousin's number. Would you please call him and ask him to send the ticket?"

"I have a better idea. Let me buy you the ticket today, and we can get you out of here tomorrow. Give me your cousin's number. I'll let him know you're coming. What is his name?"

"Salvador. Everyone calls him Chava."

"Good. I'll call him today," says my ma.

"Esperanza, do you believe what Alex said to me, about the invisible eye? Can people follow you around that way?"

"She's crazy. Jealous. Worse than a man, because she should know better. You have to leave. You should worry about that, not some magic eye." Delia is quiet for a moment, then she says, "You're right." My ma calls to me.

"Gordo, you can stop pretending to work and go get a paper and pencil for Delia."

"Okay, Ma," I say. Dang. I thought I was pretty slick, listening to them. I go into the house and get my notepad and a pencil. I bring it to Ma, and she folds it in half like a taco with the pencil in the middle and pushes it through the hole in the fence.

"Here, Delia," says Ma. "Write down his full name and his phone. I'll call him and let him know we're sending you to Chicago."

"Gracias, Esperanza. May God reward you. We'll send money back to—"

"Don't worry about it for now. Just get the hell out of that loca's prison."

"I know it's hard to understand, but I loved her."

"Everybody makes bad choices sometimes. You're pretty. You're young. You're a good person. Now look at her. What's so great about her? She's not nice to you. She has bad character. And that face of hers doesn't help either. Find a nice man in Chicago and settle down."

"That's not for me."

"A good man would be so good for you. A good one can protect you. You could start a family."

"That's not what I want," says Delia.

"Okay, mija. Go find a woman but no more brujas locas."

"Maybe it's better to be alone."

"Alone? That is the most sensible thing I've ever heard you say."

*　*　*

Me and Ma go to Salinas where the big Greyhound bus station is. I translate for Ma, like always.

"Excuse me, mister. Do you have buses to Chicago?"

"Yes. We have two buses leaving for Chicago. Let's see . . . they leave every day at seven in the morning and again at two in the afternoon." I explain to Ma, and she tells me to order one for the afternoon bus.

"How much is the two o'clock bus ticket?"

"It costs sixty-five dollars," says the ticket man. I look at my ma to translate, but I remember she understands numbers. She opens up her purse and pulls out some twenties and pays.

Ma tries out her English with the Greyhound man.

"How machi time it take, the Cheecago bas?"

"Let's see. With all the stops, it takes two and a half days."

"The bus stations having toilets?"

"Yes. And the bus has a bathroom too." Ma looks at me. She is confused. I translate. Her eyebrows go up like she's surprised. I'm surprised too. The ticket guy looks at us. He probably thinks we're dumb Mexicans who don't know nothing, but I can't help it if I look surprised. I never thought you could poop on the bus. You can't poop on the school bus. We thank the man and take Delia's ticket.

When we get back to the house, Ma goes right to the fence and talks to Delia. They talk for like twenty minutes, but I can't hear what they're saying. When Ma comes back into the house, I have to know what is happening.

"Is she ready to leave for Chicago?" I ask.

"Yes," says Ma. "Delia is going to pack her things tomorrow as soon as Alex leaves for work in the morning. A couple of suitcases and boxes. Then your Tio Hector is coming, and he's going to help her get her stuff out, drive her to the Greyhound, and get her out of that prison."

"What if Alex returns home while we're trying to escape?"

"Alex won't, because she'll be at work."

"But what if Alex gets a feeling something is happening and she returns home and catches us?"

"If that happens," says Ma, "your Tio Hector will have to beat up Alex and escape."

"What if Alex has a rifle?"

"Alex won't have a gun. But I'll tell Hector to bring his machete, just in case."

"Ma, you can't fight a gun with a machete."

"That's enough, Gordo. No more crazy gun talk. Delia is going to escape, and we're going to help her."

That night, it takes a long time to fall asleep. I have a bad dream. I'm lying in bed reading comic books and suddenly I see a blue light in the room. It's a big giant eye, floating in the air like a balloon. When it moves, it sounds like Darth Vader's light saver. I know it's the eye Alex uses to spy on

Delia, the jealous bruja eye that never sleeps. I know it's angry at me. I jump out of bed and run to get out of the room, but the eye moves fast like a humingbird and gets between me and the door. I grab a broomstick that's leaning in the corner like a baseball bat and swing at the eye. I swing and swing like some dumb kid trying to hit a jumpy piñata, but the eye zooms around so fast, I never hit it. It corners me. I jump at it and grab it in a bear hug. I hear an awful sound like when like when Grandpa stabs the long knife into a pig's throat to kill it for Christmas tamales. I wake up. I look around and I know there's no giant eye, but I still feel scared. It felt so real.

The next morning, I get up before the alarm clock. I hear my ma and pa get up. I smell Ma's coffee and the tortillas and beef she is cooking to make Pa's lunch. I hear Pa get in his truck and drive away to work. I stay in bed as the sun comes up, listening for Alex's truck leaving. When I hear some noises over the fence, I peek out the window. It's Alex. She gets in her truck and turns it on to let it warm up before she leaves. I can see her at the front fence. She's unlocking the chain and opening up the front gate. She goes back into the house and returns to the car with her silver lunch pail. She pulls the Toyota out to the street and she wraps the chain around the gate and locks it up. Then she leaves.

I walk into the kitchen and Ma is standing by the window. She's also been watching.

"She's gone," says Ma, opening the curtains.

"You think Alex will come back?" I ask.

"It's time to help Delia. C'mon."

We go to the fence. Delia is already there.

"Are you ready, Delia?" asks Ma.

"Ay, señora. I can't. This'll never work. I'm scared."

"Ay, mija. Of course you're scared, but you have to do it anyways," says Ma. "We're here to help you. My brother Hector will arrive in ten minutes when I call him, and we can get you out of here."

"I can't. I'm sorry. She's a bruja. Who knows what she'll do to me, to my family, or to you for helping me."

"Whatever she does, it won't be worse than what she already did to you. You have a good future ahead of you, Delia, but you have to escape. We support you. Your cousin is so worried about you. He loves you, and he's waiting for you in Chicago. Go get your things now."

"But there's so much stuff. I couldn't pack yesterday because she'd get suspicious."

"Quickly pack the most important things in two suitcases. A jacket and sweaters for the cold. Your papers. Your money. Toothbrush and toothpaste for the long bus ride. Family pictures. If something doesn't fit in your suitcase, leave it. You can always replace your things in Chicago. You can do it."

"Okay," says Delia.

"Good girl! Go get packed while I call my brother." Ma goes back into the house and calls Tio Hector, and in fifteen minutes he turns up, whistling like nothing is happening.

"Hola, mi Gordo!" he says to me. He gives me a big hug and pats my back hard.

"Look how big you're getting," he says to me. "You're almost taller than me." I'm so glad he's here. I feel braver already. We take him to the front gate of Alex's house, and Delia comes out. When Tio Hector sees her, he says "wow" very quietly. She comes to the fence, and my ma introduces them.

"Are you almost ready?" asks Ma.

"Almost," says Delia.

"Okay," says tio. "I'll take care of this chain in the meantime. C'mon, Gordo." Tio Hector and me go back to his little red Pinto and he opens up the back. Inside there is a big blue gym bag, and he grabs it. We walk back to Delia's driveway. Tio Hector puts the bag down. He looks up and down Hudson Street.

"Gordo, if you see a car coming, tell me. We don't want anyone to see me cutting this chain." He unzips the bag. Inside there is a machete with a taped-up handle and giant orange scissor thingies, like the ones my pa uses to cut the branches on our apple tree in the winter.

"What's that?" I ask.

"Bolt cutters," he says. "I can cut chains with this baby." He looks up and down the street one more time, grabs the chain with the tip of the scissors, and presses down. Nothing happens. He tries harder. The muscles in his neck pop out, but nothing happens.

"Hijo de puta!" he says to the chain. He tries again. He spreads his legs open and presses down hard on the bolt cutters. His arms are shaking. I hear *click*, and the chain drops. Wow. Tio Hector almost shit a brick, but he did it! He takes the chain off the gate and opens it up. In the backyard, Choco starts barking. We go over to Alex's door. It is open, but my tio knocks anyways.

"Are you ready, señorita?" he asks Delia.

"Almost," says Delia from inside.

"We should go now."

"Please come in and take these," says Delia. We go into the house. I feel scared being in Alex's house. There is a picture of her and Delia taped to the wall. They look pretty happy, but I feel like Alex is watching me. Delia has two suitcases that are stuffed like fat chorizos. There is already one box wrapped with silver tape, and she is taping up another one. Tio Hector takes the suitcases, and I take the first box, while Delia finishes taping.

We load up Delia's stuff in his Pinto and walk back to her house. Tio Hector picks up the last box. Delia looks through her purse, zips it up, and puts it on her shoulder. We go out, and she locks the door. Choco is barking, so Delia goes and kneels next to him. His tail is wagging, and he is licking her face. She hugs him around the neck and kisses his forehead. As she walks to us, I can see that her eyes are wet. Delia grabs a broom from the deck. *Whoosh, whoosh, whoosh.* She starts to sweep away our footprints in the dirt. She walks backward and makes all the footprints disappear. My tio is watching her; he looks sideways at me. I can tell he thinks this is weird. I do too, but I understand now. Alex is a really bad person.

Delia has to disappear so good that even Encyclopedia Brown couldn't figure out how she did it. At the end of the driveway, Delia finally closes the gate.

"Let's start this adventure," says Tio Hector. He's smiling like we're going to Disneyland or something. Delia smiles a little bit too, but she doesn't look happy. We walk up Hudson Street to our house. My ma is waiting by the Pinto.

"We should go now," says my tio.

"Wait," says Ma. She goes into the house and comes back with a little brown bag in one hand and a necklace in her other hand. She stands face-to-face in front of Delia.

"Here are some burritos to eat on the bus when you get hungry. You need blessings, hija. Benedictions," says Ma. Delia puts her hands together to pray, looks down, and closes her eyes. Ma puts the necklace around Delia's neck and pulls Delia's long hair over the necklace.

"This is Saint Christopher. He'll watch over your travels," says Ma.

"Now give me your hand." Delia lifts up her hand, and Ma slides a little blue bracelet on Delia's wrist. It has a silver hand with an eye on it.

"This is the eye of Fatima, to protect you from the evil eye."

Ma begins praying the Ave Maria. She does the sign of the cross on Delia, the big sign. She goes from Delia's forehead to her belly button to her shoulders. Then she draws a circle in the air around Delia. Then she does it again, praying and praying. Delia's back begins to shake. Ma does the sign of the cross again, and Delia covers her face and cries really hard but quietly, like she doesn't want to bother anyone. Ma hugs her, and Delia holds on to Ma like she is drowning and Ma's gonna save her. Ma puts her hands on Delia's cheeks and lifts up her face. Their noses are almost kissing.

"Go and be happy," says Ma. "It snows there in Chicago. Go see the snow. Have you ever seen it?"

"Only on television."

"Can you imagine how pretty the snow will be? Like a movie." Ma smiles. I can almost believe it's gonna be okay. Delia wipes her wet face with the back of her hand. Ma kisses her on the forehead.

"Ready to go?" asks Tio Hector.

"I'm ready." They get into Tio Hector's little red car. He backs out of the driveway. We wave and wave at Delia, and she waves once. The car pulls away, and she's gone.

Me and Ma stand in the driveway. Delia's gone. I don't know what to do. But Ma knows. I look up at her. Her mouth is moving. I can barely hear her, but I know she is praying hard.

O clement, O loving, O sweet Virgin.
To thee do we cry, poor banished children of Eve.
Protect her.
Protect her like a mother.

Spread your green cloak with the gold stars and
wrap it around her.
Hide her from the evil eyes that will search for
her to hurt her.
Protect her, Holy Queen, Mother of Mercy, our
life, our sweetness, our gracious advocate, and
our hope.
Amen.

"Amen," I say. "I never heard that prayer before."

"I made some of it up. Let's hope it works, mijo."

It felt good to help Delia escape in the morning, but all day long I feel like something bad is gonna happen, like a big black rock is sitting at the bottom of my stomach. I close the curtains on the two windows that face Alex's house. Around 4:30 p.m., I get more and more nervous. Alex is gonna be home soon. I open the curtains, but only an inch, to spy on Alex's place and see if she's home from work.

When I see her rusty pickup coming up Hudson Street, my heart is like a big fist, trying to break out of my chest. Alex gets out of her truck to open the gate. She sees the broken chain and stops. I stop breathing. She jogs to the door and pulls out her keys so fast she drops them. She opens the door.

"Gordo!" says Ma. I jump. I step back from the window.

"Jesus, Ma! You almost gave me a heart attack. I was looking to see when Alex got home."

"You don't worry about Alex and get away from that window." I step away. She opens the curtains wide open.

"Don't, Ma! Close the curtains. What if she comes here to our house?"

"Of course she is going to come. Sylvie, come here now!" says Ma. Sylvie walks into the room. "Listen carefully, both of you. If Alex asks you about Delia, you didn't see anything, you don't know anything. You were both with me all day at your nana's in San Juan Bautista. We went to Lucky's and then to McDonald's and then the Goodwill. That's the story, okay?"

"Okay," we both say.

"I'll do the talking. You stay quiet. Now go watch TV or read or something and stop spying." Sylvie goes outside, and I go to the living room sofa and pick up *Encyclopedia Brown Saves the Day*. He's my favorite, but when I read a sentence, I can't remember what I just read. I keep trying to read, but nothing is making sense. I close the book and turn on the TV instead. It's *Bewitched*. Samantha's funny Uncle Arthur is on the show today. He's the best, but I'm too nervous to have fun watching him. Ma starts cooking. Time goes super slow. I smell onions cooking, then meat, then chilis. My stomach makes a small animal noise I've never heard before. I watch the clock. If Alex comes to our house looking for Delia, I hope Pa is home by then. He'll send her down a tube if she tries to hit anybody or say things.

Pa usually gets home by 5:30 p.m., maybe 6:00 p.m., unless he's drinking or went to Lucky's.

Ma tells me and Sylvie to eat. It's refried beans, tortillas, and chili con carne. I'm eating my food when I hear the knock on the door. Sylvie says, "Uh-oh." I want to lock the door and hide, but instead, I gotta pretend everything is normal. Ma nods at me. I nod back at her. I hear Ma open the door.

"Hola, Esperanza."

"Hola, Alex," says Ma.

"Esperanza. Do you have a moment?"

"Yes, come in," says Ma. "Come and eat with us."

"Thank you, but I'm not hungry."

"How about coffee then?"

"Coffee would be good."

Alex comes in looking like she ate poison.

"Gordo," she says.

"Hi, Alex," I say, trying to sound cheerful.

"Let me get your coffee," says my ma. She pours a cup for Alex.

"Would you like—"

"Black. Please. I like it black," says Alex. Ma passes Alex the cup of coffee.

"You don't look so good, Alex. Are you okay?" asks Ma.

"I came home and that cabrona Delia is gone," says Alex.

"What?" says Ma, covering her mouth with her hand. "What do you mean she's gone? Where'd she go?"

"I don't know."

"Maybe she went to do some errands," says Ma.

"No. She left a note. She said she was leaving forever and don't look for her."

"Oh my goodness, that is so terrible. I'm sorry, Alex. You must be feeling so bad." Alex nods her head, and her eyes get teary.

"After everything I did for her. She was escaping from hell. I opened my doors to her."

"Yes, you were very good to her, Alex," says Ma.

"Everything she needed, I gave her," says Alex. "Food. A home. Clothes. A safe place to live. She didn't even have to work."

"Ay ay ay," says Ma.

"I thought she'd stay forever, but now she's gone."

"You must be so sad."

"Yes. I'm sad. And I'm mad too. But this is not the end of the story, Esperanza." Alex's face looks hard now. Alex points at her own eyes with two fingers.

"I can see things, señora. I can see things that other people can't see. I sat there in the empty room, I asked it what happened. And I saw him."

"Saw who?"

"Her man. Her sancho. Pfft. He's not much of a man. I saw him short. I saw him curly haired. Black hair. Mustache. Piece of shit tiny car. Blue car." Oh my God. The man she saw in her head is my Tio Hector. Except for the car color, that's him exactly! How could she know?

Ma pushes back her hair behind her ear and touches her neck. I wish Pa was here. Alex was at work all day. How did she see Tio Hector? Was it with the evil eye that's gonna follow Delia to Chicago?

I look around and try to figure out what I can hit Alex with if she gets out of control. What do you use to hit an angry witch? The broomstick! I'll whack her across her face with the broomstick if I have to. Nobody hassles my ma. Except Pa.

"When I find her," says Alex, "she's going to pay. That sancho is going to pay too. On that day, she will finally know who I truly am. What I am capable of. If you're good to me, I'm good to you. But if you're bad to me . . ."

"Ay, Alex," says Ma. "She left you. I'm so sorry."

"Did you see anything, Esperanza?" asks Alex. Ma breathes in with her nose. She looks Alex right in the eyes.

"No. I didn't see anything. I was out with Sylvie and Gordo most of the day. Groceries. Visiting my mother. Trip to the Goodwill like always."

"Before you left, did you see anything suspicious?" asks Alex again. "Did Delia ever say anything to you about leaving?"

"Me and Delia hardly ever talked. When we did, she would always be talking about her country, her family. She seemed so homesick, but I thought she was happy. Who knows why people do what they do? I know it was bad over there in El Salvador, but that is where her blood is. No matter what happens, the blood calls to you. Maybe she went back home to her country."

"So you saw nothing?" asks Alex.

"Gordo," Alex says. "How about you? Did you see anything? A man who came to my house and left with that bitch?" I try to gulp, but now there's a baseball in my throat.

"No. I don't think so." My voice is tiny.

"What do you mean, you don't think so?" asks Alex. She is looking at me hard.

"He was with me all day," says Ma.

"He ate two Big Macs for lunch at McDonald's," says Sylvie.

"You're my neighbors," says Alex. "And I trust you." She looks right into my eyes. My face is burning.

"If you remember anything," says Alex, "I hope you'll tell me right away. I'll find her one way or another. I saw the place she's gone to. Probably Soledad, maybe Salinas. I saw a taqueria in the barrio. I can find her on my own, but I hope you'll tell me if you remember anything. Thank you for the coffee." Alex stands up suddenly. I'm ready to grab the broom.

"Goodbye, neighbors," says Alex.

"Goodbye, Alex," says Ma.

Alex walks out. We hear the door close. We hear her walking down the driveway.

"Stay right where you are," says Ma. She runs to the bedroom. I hear her opening the sliding closet doors. I hear her moving things. She comes back with a small glass bottle. She takes off the lid and swings the bottle at me and Sylvie, sprinkling us with the water.

"Hey, what are you doing, Ma?" I ask.

"Shhh. This is holy water. Blessed by the archbishop of Guadalajara at the Basilica of Our Lady of Zapopan. Nothing is stronger than this water. Not even her brujería." Ma sprinkles some on herself. She does the sign of the cross on me and Sylvie and then on herself. "There. We're protected now. Delia is far away now. That witch is all alone, except for poor Choco. If that dog ever says he wants to escape that fat bruja, we'll help him too." We all start to laugh hard, and I feel like I'm never gonna stop.

"Ay, Ma," says Sylvie. "That's crazy, about Choco escaping."

"Crazy, crazy, crazy, but you're laughing, laughing, laughing."

That night at bedtime, after I shut the lights, I hear Choco bark a few times in the dark. I peek through the curtains. I can't see the moon behind the fat clouds. I look at Alex's house. I see a tiny orange glow near the back door. It's the cherry of Alex's cigarette. She's standing there, smoking in the dark. I can't see her face, only her outline. She is a shadow, a man's shadow, blacker than the night. A big dog shadow walks to her, and they become one thing.

I see her other arm go up, holding a long bottle of El Máximo. She drinks from the bottle, then she takes another puff. She puts her head back and looks up at the clouds for a moment, then she looks at my window. Shit! She is looking right at me! I can feel my heart beating, but it's beating in my back. She can see in the dark, like an owl. No. She can't. It's dark outside, and it's even darker in this room. I only opened the curtain a tiny crack. No one can see me, not even her. It only looks like she's looking at me spying on her. She watches our house and doesn't move. I can't move either. It's like a spell. I can't breathe. I can't stop looking. I'm becoming a statue.

"Hey, stop spying," whispers Sylvie from her bed in the room.

"Leave me alone," I whisper. I sound annoyed, but I'm glad she talked and broke the spell that was making me into a statue. I back away from the window slowly, till I feel my bed with the back of my legs. I lie down in bed and pull the blankets up to my chin.

"What did you see?" asks Sylvie.

"Just Alex and Choco."

"You and Mom helped Delia escape today," says Sylvie.

"Yeah."

"You helped someone," says Sylvie. "That was cool."

"Thanks," I say. I lay in bed with my eyes open. I hear an owl.

I want to turn on the lights.

I want to ask my Magic 8-Ball if Alex saw me in the dark.

I want to ask Sylvie to play Uno with me till I get sleepy.

I want to take my blankets and my pillow and go sleep on the floor in Ma and Pa's bedroom, next to the heater that makes a nice sound.

But I don't.

I close my eyes. I don't want to think about Alex, so I try to think of Delia instead. At first, I can't picture her, but then

I see her. I see her sitting in a Greyhound bus. It is almost morning outside, and the bus has lights inside. I see Delia covered in a blanket all the way to her chin, like me. The blanket is green, with tiny gold stars. She's sleeping and has a little smile on her face like she is having a nice dream about snow covering everything and making it new.

The Pardos

The ecosystem of every town requires at least one bad family. If a town doesn't have a true bad family, it will regularly elevate a somewhat troubled family to bad family status. Watsonville has a bona fide bad family in the Pardos. Most people who know Nelson Pardo or his sons tend to believe the story that he had killed his wife back in El Salvador. The rumor is rumored to have been started by the only other Salvadoran family in town. As the story passes through the rumor mill, it grows and evolves. Garish details are confected, added, and spiced up to taste. Over time, the conjecture gels into a gospel well known to the students at Callaghan High School. The core of the gospel says that Colonel Pardo was an officer in the Salvadoran army and the ill-fated, unnamed wife was the daughter of a powerful banana-growing family. When Coronel Pardo expressed an interest in the middle daughter, Mariana, the family said yes and married off the girl of nineteen to curry favor with the military. In less than three years, she birthed three sons and loved them dearly. She also loved a journalist and met with him secretly. When Nelson learned of this, Mariana promptly became one of The Disappeared whose absence would haunt the country. The state of her mangled corpse was such that a closed-casket funeral was necessary. Nelson did not pretend to cry at the funeral, and within a week, he was quite recovered and chipper, eyeing with hot interest the adolescent muchacha they hired to help with the three boys.

Mr. Pardo knows of the rumors. He has never shared details of his life that might explain away the dark accusations, mitigate the fear and suspicion of his neighbors. He likes it that way. Back in El Salvador, he had some power within a rogue military. Everyone was rightfully afraid of any officer. The poorest Mayan peasants, shopkeepers, suited elites—all of them knew to fear, bribe, and cater to men like Nelson. Since immigrating to California with his sons, he has labored as a night janitor at the Jolly Giant plant, humping great wheelbarrows of broccoli clippings left behind by the mostly Mexican women who worked the vegetable-processing lines.

As he pitches heaping shovels of stems and leaves, he imagines the hated women, lined up overhead like squat birds on power lines, endlessly squawking and launching green droppings behind them to land on the floor below where he and other worker ants toil through the night, their passing marked only by the dumpsters they leave piled high with wilting vegetable clippings.

At home, Nelson's long showers never quite remove the chlorophyll stink of his downfall. Broccoli. Spinach. Cauliflower. They offend his nose, but worst of all are the brussels sprouts.

"Fucking puto brussels," he hisses behind the wheelbarrow. "Those people in Brussels must be assholes to make this asshole vegetable. Who eats these fuckers, anyways?"

He sleeps till noon, and by the time he wakes up, his sons are in school and the house is empty. He lounges on his lumpy recliner and flips through the channels. The color television cost him more than his used pickup truck, but it was worth it. It is the one thing in his life that does exactly what he wants, every time. The television's high-ticket presence is anomalous in the ramshackle living room. A semicircle of battered, mismatched chairs surround it, as if marveling at its glowing newness. As a night worker, he ends up watching daytime television. After almost a decade in this country, he has learned some English—not enough to understand everything he is seeing, but he has clear preferences. He likes the wild animal programs and the cartoons. He cannot much tolerate the soaps, talk shows, and dramas. His deepest loathing is reserved for the endlessly talking, weeping, emoting women who reign over the afternoon programs.

For all his dissatisfaction, he likes the hypnotic passage of images, the weight of the remote in his hand, which makes him feel as one with his television. As he cycles through the five channels, he imagines the day of liberation, when he finally walks away from his lowly work, never again to deal with the hated line women, the truckloads of vegetables, the Jolly Giant corporation, or the unknowable final consumers of the brussels sprouts who drive the whole accursed scenario.

For reassurance, Nelson unpacks memories of El Salvador and polishes them like family silver. He remembers the moist density of the warm air, the hum and purple flash of colibrí hovering in the garden, and the emerald cast on everything beneath the tree canopy. He remembers that he was considered a tall man in El Salvador. His nostalgia of El Salvador is rigidly compartmentalized, sealing off the beautiful from everything else. Even so, the darker memories infiltrate the reveries, and he remembers. The crack of gunshots. The screams of the defiant guerrillas and ill-starred civilians. The useless pleas for mercy and claims of innocence of those peasant indios. To be at once so powerless and so unbreakable made them equally infuriating and frightening.

"Like animals, they were," he announces to the circled jury of chairs. "And what happened had to happen. Nothing to be done about it now." He works the cap off his Budweiser with a quarter, drinks deeply, and doesn't bother to wipe it off when it runs down his chin.

The loss of Indians and peasants to terrorize leave him with only his boys.

*   *   *

It is obvious the boys have not had a mother in a while. At Callaghan High School they are the lowest order of cholos, lacking the elaborate grooming, precisely creased pants, and spit shined shoes of their homeys. Inveterate brawlers, they fight constantly at home. The bloody battles are waged over television-viewing rights, snacks, one-on-one basketball calls, and most everything else the brothers do together. Nelson is not bothered by his sons' fights, but if he gets a whiff of insubordination from any of them, he marches all of them out to the garage to witness the punishment. Nelson hooks the offending boy up to a crude electric circuit powered by a Sears DieHard battery. The hapless boy must hold a naked copper wire in each hand, while his father sits at the switch and flicks it on and off.

"How you like it, hojoeputa?" he asks. The boys grimace and twitch with each surge of electricity. None of them has ever figured out how to answer that question.

Spooky, the oldest of the Pardo boys, has been in juvenile detention for almost a year. The two younger brothers, Tinman and Shy Boy, are fully expected to join him by fellow students and teachers alike. The brothers are all legal immigrants, courtesy of their father's connections back home, but their true citizenship takes the form of Chicano alienation. They sport shaved heads and shoddy homemade tattoos on their arms. It is 1981, and that is far more than a fashion statement. Spooky landed at Callaghan High School as fierce as a Cossack. The scowling boy seemed to fear no one, even when it would have been wise to be afraid. Within a few days, Spooky began building the Pardo family reputation.

On that day, Tank Brodovich strode down the hall enjoying the view over everyone's heads, and happy to be done with the school day. On the narrow sidewalk leading to the student parking lot, clusters of freshmen parted before him and re-formed in his wake. All was as it should be. Spooky walked toward him in the opposite. As they neared and their eyes met. Neither boy stepped to the side to avoid the other, and they bumped shoulders.

"Watch where you're goin', honkey beech," hissed Spooky. Of the four Pardo brothers, Spooky had been the slowest to pick up the English language, but he knew enough to form and hurl a basic insult. Tank was taken aback by the audacity of Spooky. He had six inches and about a hundred pounds on this fucker.

"You watch it, runt," spat Tank.

The fight was legendary. Spooky fought jungle style, a desperate and undisciplined style. Tank curled his beefy, furred fists and pounded Spooky's face and body, but Spooky just kept coming back. One, two, three times he rose from the sidewalk to continue. Swinging high to reach Tank's face, Spooky had no body behind his blows, and they landed ineffectually, grazing Tank's skull, neck, and shoulders. By the end of the fight, Spooky's face was busted out at the mouth, nose, and eyes. A red constellation of specks and streaks spread across his T-shirt. Pinned to the wall by the school security officers, Spooky glared at Tank and spit out a bloody chain of curses through his split lips. Tank was unhurt and victorious, and he walked away with his football friend Gus.

"You okay, dude?" asked Gus.

"Yeah, I'm fine. He didn't get in a good hit."

"You fucked him up good, Tank."

"Gus, did you see his eyes?" asked Tank.

"Yeah, I saw them. Crazy eyes."

"I'd rather fight three normal dudes at once than have to fight that crazy little shit again."

All of the Pardo brothers have struggled to settle into California life, but it's been hard. Time spent in Callaghan High School is a rather soft but tedious sentence they must serve. They have no friends and never date. Occasionally a girl will favor one of them with a perfunctory hi, a wave, or a subtle upward tilting of the head, but that is the extent of their attention. While the brothers sit together during lunchtime, the girls stroll past them in packs, cool as November. The girls chat at intimate volumes, sizing up the unkempt Pardos.

"Nice shoes they got," says one hawk-eyed girl.

"Attention Kmart shoppers," announces the pretty Divina Sanchez, forming a megaphone around her mouth with her hands and whispering hoarsely. "We are having a blue

light special on cheap ol' fake tennies in the shoe depart-
ment." Laughter.

"Too bad they don't have a sale on soap, cuz those vatos
need it baaad!" added Rosie Archebeque.

"Stop faking it, Rosie," says Divina. "Everybody knows
you're in love with Shy Boy."

"Hell no, I'm not," counters Rosie. "I need a man, and
that vato looks like a sixth grader. I'm not a child molester,
homey. Besides, what am I supposed to do with that shrimp?"
The girls laugh again.

Adjusting to life away from El Salvador has been hard. Back
at their sprawling home in the capital city of San Salvador, the
maid would tell Tinman that he was the best-looking of the
family. The reddish Mayan color, prominent hooked nose, and
straight hair of his father bypassed him. Like his late mother,
he has hazel eyes and thick eyelashes. Tinman's skin is on
the lighter end of the mestizo spectrum. A light brown that
is not quite prized but also not disdained. Praise is rarely on
offer back in the Pardo home, especially after they buried the
mother, and Tinman has never forgotten that the maid had
told him he was handsome, entitled to attention and company.
Tinman keeps his eyes open for the just-right girl, not too
pretty, not too ugly, not too confident. A girl who maybe has
just one great thing, like a nice smile or big breasts. He tries
repeatedly to connect with one girl, freckled and green-eyed,
with whom he shares a history class.

"Hi Sylvia."

"My name is Sylvie, not Sylvia."

"Oh darned. Sorry about that, Sylvie. Sooo. How are you doing, aye?"

"I'm cool, thanks."

"Hey, can I walk with you to gym class?"

"Sorry, but I'm in kind of a hurry. Mrs. Mitchell the Bitchell is my PE teacher, and if you're late, she'll make you run laps. See you later, okay?"

"Okay. Later. Have a good PE, okay?"

"Thanks."

"I'll see you around, okay, Sylvie."

"See you."

At night, on the mattress, on the floor, he waits for the soft snoring of Shy Boy at his side, turns his back, closes his eyes, conjures Sylvia, and quietly masturbates. It doesn't take long. His breath catches and he cums in waves that ripple through him and leave him spent. He rises and washes his hand at the bathroom sink. Returning to bed, he immediately descends into sleep with his hand in his briefs, cradling his penis.

In all of Callaghan High School, only the cafeteria ladies are fond of Tinman, and Shy Boy. Lined up at the lunchroom steam tables in hairnets and aprons, the ladies are tough and practical but also ready to serve up a bit of salty-sweet surrogate mothering with each upturned scoop of food they drop into the compartments of the plastic lunch trays. Some of the ladies had raised sons of their own and were familiar with the blustery way of boys. They watch with dismay and disgust as the students of Callaghan High School daily discard vast amounts of half-eaten food. Some found this disposal an insult to their work in the kitchen. The Pardo boys were different from those wasteful kids. Even by teenager standards, the boys were prodigious eaters. Chicken a la king, sloppy joes, tacos, raisin-carrot salad, and even the spinach, boiled beyond recognition, are wolfed down with uniform gusto by the brothers. They eat in silence, heads bowed over their putty-colored trays, sporks held baby-style in their fists, which rise and fall mechanically. When they finish, the boys take the trays back to the cafeteria line. Their eyes are bright and urgent. Tinman smiles and asks, "Can we please have more, please?"

"We only have corn left if that's okay," says one of the ladies.

"Yeah, please, your corn's really good."

The praise dignifies the ladies' work, but more than that, a hungry mouth opens something up in them, a generosity. The ladies pile it on, filling each compartment of the trays with little pyramids of corn.

"Thank you."

"You're welcome." By the time the Pardos have gotten seconds, many of their fellow students have cleared out, and the boys have the cafeteria mostly to themselves. They quietly hunch over their trays and disappear the food, wiping the buttery sauce with their last bits of bread.

*   *   *

After lunch, they sit on the gym steps, mostly watching the flow of students go by, sometimes sharpening their sporks into makeshift daggers by rubbing them against the sidewalk. A cheap cassette player between Tinman's feet plays oldies they recorded off the radio. To the scratchy keening of Rosie and the Originals, they wait for the bell and the classes they may or may not attend according to their moods. Their grades are uniformly poor, but the Pardos don't mind. They have accepted that school is not for them. Even in woodshop and auto maintenance, where many boys with academic allergies can experience success and satisfaction, the Pardos refuse to be inspired. Shy Boy can take apart, adjust, and then reassemble a carburetor, but he can't pass the simplest yes/no auto shop quiz. So the brothers do their time in school and wait for something to happen. Expulsion. Flunking out. Dropping out. Something.

In class, Shy Boy sits in the back row and cultivates invisibility, hiding behind unread books covered in brown grocery bag paper. His spiral binder is illuminated with page upon page of ballpoint drawings. Delicate vine roses arch over long-necked peacocks. Sacred hearts crowned in thorns burn away. He draws his neighbors' shoes, capturing the glint off the patent leather and texturing the shoelaces with feathery crosshatching. As he falls ever more behind in his classes, Shy Boy's ballpoint technique blossoms. At times he shocks himself with the richness of his work. The roses grow ever more graceful. His horse threatens to gallop off the page. Anything is possible in Shy Boy's notebook, except algebra.

In his classes, Shy Boy is in particular trouble. He arrived in the United States and began learning English at a younger age than his older brothers, but his English is the most halting and cautious. He understands it, but when he tries to speak, the words scatter, hiding in burrows and mocking him. The teachers slow down and try to help. It is exquisitely embarrassing.

"If you're not sure of the answer, can you take a guess?"
Silence.

"What do you think the answer might be? Try, just try."
Silence.

"It's okay if you don't get it right. We can learn from our mistakes. I make mistakes all the time."

"Sorry. I don't know."

I'll never belong here, he thinks.

Shy Boy never stops yearning for his tropics. He never stops yearning for Profesora Hernandez and that starchy cotton solidarity of his uniformed schoolmates. Shy Boy's distant memories of his mother are fragmented and painfully elusive. He was so young when she joined The Disappeared. Still, he remembers a kiss from her, on his forehead. The memory does not have her words in it, nor her face, but it conjures in Shy Boy a yearning as imperishably lustrous as a gold ingot.

As the teacher's lecture and explain, Shy Boy is distracted, writing and rewriting his name, his true name.

"Mauricio" horizontally in cursive.

"Mauricio" upside down.

"Mauricio" in a spiral.

"Mauricio" progressively fading to almost nothing between the first letter and the last.

And finally, "Mauricio" standing tall in a jungle of palm trees. The "M" is sturdy, with sinewy roots clinging to the soil. The tips of the "M" reach above the palm trees and branch out like grasping fingers reaching for a clear, Salvadoran sky.

The Problem of Style

I n the summer after sixth grade, as he crossed the creaking vine-and-slat suspension bridge toward the overgrown wilds of San Benito Junior High, Raymundo decided he was going to become art. Maybe not art exactly but more *artistic*. He grew his hair out longer and longer. In much of the United States, it was the seventies, but in San Benito County farm towns, home of farmworkers fresh from rural Mexico and sunburnt ranchers just a generation removed from the Oklahoma Dust Bowl, it was simultaneously the fifties. The teacher's room of the middle school was a temporal anomaly, where time seemed to have looped back on itself. The fifties, sixties, and seventies lay in perplexing proximity to each other, like the empty rum bottles, dead seagulls, tree branches, and Barbie doll heads that commingle on beaches after epic storms.

San Benito Junior High's veteran teachers like Mr. Tackwater watched the newly minted teachers with suspicion, daily gathering and cross-referencing intelligence. He noted it all: their loud frocks and unkempt serial-murderer sideburns, their tepid patriotism, their fussy firework proclamations about the importance of student autonomy and critical thinking, as if seventh graders knew shit from proverbial Shinola, as if immigrant children could become Americans without American guidance.

He suspected the younger teachers secretly mocked him, saluting the flag like he meant it, dressing professionally with his chest and nuts roasting in the hotbox fire of his polyblend suits. He imagined they were colluding against him when he saw groups of those soft, shaggy not-quite-men and the tight little covens of sob sisters in their ponchos and culottes. The Baptist ramrod ladies he first taught with in the midfifties would have snapped these gals over their righteous knees. Thank God most of those early teachers had gone to their reward or were retired, so they didn't have to see this generation of teachers flush all these poor kids down the toilet.

On the first day of school, rows of boys sat cross-legged on the shiny gym floor. Mr. Tackwater paced and watched as the last of them trickled in and he noted the androgynous blemish that was Raymundo sandwiched in between two freshly crew cut boys. He caught the boy's eye and called him over with his crooked finger. Raymundo rose with a look of concern and came to Mr. Tackwater.

"Son, what is your name?"

"Raymundo Sanchez."

"Well, Mr. Sanchez, I'm Mr. Tackwater, and I want to know what exactly you are planning with that hair."

"I don't have plans, I think."

"Are you trying to be a hippie, Mr. Sanchez?"

"I like it this way, sir. It's not against the rules, is it?"

"No, unfortunately it is not. You seem to be a bright kid. Polite. I wouldn't want you to ruin all that with this hair of yours."

"I won't, sir. It's not anything bad. It's just my style."

"That's the point, son. Talk to your daddy. Ask him what people think about boys who run around worrying about their style. It could open your eyes. You might be surprised."

"Okay. I will."

Raymundo's schoolmates, those boys he'd known since kindergarten, saw his changed appearance and suddenly knew him differently. Raymundo had left sixth grade a quiet boy who played tetherball at lunch, sometimes by himself. He was rarely hassled. Raymundo was a kid sighted out of the corner of one's eye, moving through school with feral caution. During that transitional summer, he would brush out his hair and savor its growing weight in the shower. At night, he curled the waves of it around his fingers, spiraling into sleep where he imagined himself gestating in a silken black cocoon. By his first day of junior high, it was down past his shoulders. His transformation was complete, he had abandoned his previous mission of invisibility, and everyone who cared to see could see he had become something new.

"Fag."

This was his name.

"Fag."

His horsehair shirt.

"Fag."

His vocation.

Fag. Once assigned to Raymundo, the word cemented itself to him with a barnacle's stubborn might. He was not ready for this designation, but taxonomy was destiny, and his faggotry now seemed to issue uncontrollably from his pores. It trailed after him: a shameful, florid perfume. In the school halls, it possessed his hips as he walked. In class, he would stare at the back of a boy's neck and the sight would bind his free will and hijack his penis with sudden violence. On the basketball courts, the boys instinctively attacked that in Raymundo that threatened something mighty but fragile in them.

"Hey, fag. How's life in Fagville today?"

He walked past in silence, grateful for the protection offered by his mirrored shades. His silence afforded no protection, and they persisted.

"I said, HEY, FAGGOT. Can't you hear me, puto?" Raymundo held his breath, patrolled his hips, and walked faster.

"Whatsamatter? You late for a date with your boyfriend?"

"Does he smack you when you're late, Raygay?"

Life got dangerous. Once and then twice, he came home with bruises and tears in his clothing. Both times the attacks paralyzed him. He had of course argued with his sister and with classmates in the past, but he had never fought before. Didn't know how, didn't see why. He tried to fight the second time it happened, but his fists felt as alien as wings. Hitting someone was as strange as flying. His mother, devastated by the severity of the beatdown, dialed to call the school, but he protested and lied, "No, Ma. It was me who started the fights. I'll get busted."

"All right. But no more fights. Period."

School changed. Each long day, he feared the violence and humiliations that could rain down on him now that he was not invisible. He spent lunchtimes in the library, finding quiet corners within sight of the protective librarians. He feigned sickness whenever he could to escape the terrors of PE and avoided the bathrooms until he could no longer hold it in. Crossing from class to class became a precisely timed scramble across enemy lines. He checked the path to his locker, left and right. If he saw trouble, he backed into the classroom and waited for the danger to pass. He sprinted to his locker and tried to get the combination in one go before racing to his next period.

Kids who had previously been friendly or at least neutral to Raymundo began to distance themselves, afraid of becoming collateral damage in an attack or being seen as a fellow traveler. His longtime homey Olga remained loyal.

"Why don't you leave him alone, ese?" asked Olga when Junior Barba harassed Raymundo.

"Why should I?" replied Junior.

"Because he didn't do nothing to you, that's why," said Olga.

"Pfft," said Junior, turning to Raymundo. "You got a girl protecting you, Raygay? What a puto. Why don't you stand up for yourself, ese?" Raymundo had no response.

"C'mon, Ray," she said. "We're going. What you said, Junior, that is messed up."

"She's tougher than you are, Raygay!" sneered Junior as they walked away.

"Hey, Olga, thanks homey," said Raymundo afterward.

"What Junior Said was messed up, Ray. But I'm not afraid of that guy."

"Thanks for helping me, Olga, but you know what? You gotta stop defending me. It only makes me look worse."

"So I'm supposed to let them push you around?" asked Olga.

"I don't know, Olga, but I'll figure it out, okay? Just let them say what they say. I can take it."

"Okay, homey, whatever you say," said Olga. "Maybe you should go ahead and fight it out with one of them so they know they can't push you around."

"I don't know how to fight," he said.

"Then just fight however you can, loco," said Olga. "Swing, kick, bite. Just to make them think twice."

"We'll see," he responded.

Raymundo took comfort in improbable peace-through-strength fantasies of beating his tormentors till they begged for a detente. He imagined running away to San Francisco, Santa Cruz, or anyplace with cafés. He imagined magically transferring to an upscale middle school with tame white children, leaving only an empty chrysalis of himself at San Benito Junior High.

Raymundo's life seemed broken to him, but his heart, eyes, and penis worked just fine. They all pointed toward beauty, which is to say toward Mateo Valenzuela. At the edge of the playground, Raymundo watched Mateo thread his way through players on the basketball court, laying up the ball so prettily that his opponents sucked their teeth and cocked their heads in admiration. And when the ball dropped in, he would smile. The mole on his cheek would rise, his teeth would flash, and he'd push his wet hair off his forehead. Raymundo watched discreetly, taking fitful glances and then pretending to focus on something else, anything else. His sneaker, the clouds, the gymnasium doors. He understood his place in the school's caste system, understood that his gaze was a contamination and an affront to Mateo, a violation of honor that required retribution.

The day that Raymundo finally felt the touch of Mateo was harrowing. School was letting out, and as Raymundo passed the portable classrooms, Mateo and his friend Joey Sandoval took him by the arms and pulled him into the walkway between the back of the portables and the cyclone fence that ringed the campus.

"Don't! Leave me alone!"

They pulled him into the space between the gym and the fence. Raymundo twisted and struggled and protested. In response, Joey bent Raymundo's arm behind his back. Mateo hovered over him.

"Yo, Mateo, if you don't mess up his face, there won't be no evidence," coached Joey.

"How come you've been lookin' at me, Raygay?" Raymundo had never seen Mateo this close before.

"I'm not looking at you," protested Raymundo. Mateo was terrible and beautiful, an avenging angel.

"Don't lie, faggot. I seen you looking. Don't be lookin' at me. You think I'm a faggot like you?"

"It's not true. I'm not that."

"Shit. You can't even say it, but you're a fuckin' fag. Now say it."

"It's not tru—"

One blow connected with Raymundo's belly. The other with his face. Raymundo froze.

"Say it, puto."

Mateo's knee snapped upward. Raymundo tried to evade by twisting to the side, but still caught some of the blow with his crotch. Raymundo bent down, sucked air, and fought back the tears.

"Say it, bitch."

"If you say so," said Raymundo, still facing the dirt. "That's what I am."

"Louder, bitch. I can't hear you." Raymundo lifted his head and met Mateo's eyes.

"Fag. I'm a fag," said Raymundo in a hoarse whisper.

The uppercut to Raymundo's chin was revelatory. He had grown up without brothers, without brawls, and had never been hit hard enough to actually see stars, but there he was, staggering to the ground like a regular boy. A great chrysanthemum of sparks erupted across his field of vision. He had always thought that only cartoon characters saw stars. This revelation seemed inexplicably comical, and he laughed.

"What are you laughing at, bitch?" asked Mateo. The laughter enveloped Raymundo protectively, shutting out everything else.

"Fuckin' faggot's crazy," muttered Joey. Raymundo laughed even more, his voice ascending into high-pitched hysteria. Mateo kicked him in the chest, and Raymundo fell back in the dirt. His head thumped against the dirt. He laughed again.

"If you *ever* look at me again," hissed Mateo, "I'll kill you, crazy bitch." As they strode away, Raymundo's laughter softened and passed into sobs. His tears blurred the world. He sat up and rubbed the back of his head. Raymundo could taste the ferrous tang of his own blood on his tongue. Mateo's dirt footprint lay across his left pectoral like a badge. Underneath the shirt, the footprint throbbed painfully.

He heard the school buses pulling up to the bus stop and stood up to catch his but changed his mind.

"I'm not getting on that bus looking like this," he proclaimed to himself. He dusted himself off and, to avoid being seen, climbed the cyclone fence and hoisted himself over the top. He headed toward the railroad tracks beyond the lettuce field that bordered the schoolyard. At the tracks, he began walking homeward. The school sounds began to fade. He pulled errant strands of hair from the clotted blood on his face. When his hips grew loose, he let them. When the breeze caught his hair, he savored it. When the song rose up in his throat, he sang it.

> *You can't crack my heart*
> *Cuz it's made of stone*
>
> *You could've loved me a little*
> *Could've thrown me a bone*
>
> *You could've loved me a little*
> *Could've thrown me a bone*
>
> *Guess I've gotta fly away*
> *One more time, baby*
>
> *This'll be the last time*
> *Till the next time, baby*

Raymundo approached his home carefully, hoping to slink in and clean himself up before his mother saw him. Standing at the kitchen sink, Chelo saw him approaching at a distance and waved. He waved back limply and stood at the door for a moment before entering. He breathed in slowly and opened the door. From the sink, Chelo turned and saw her son.

"Oh Jesus! What happened to your face now, mijo?" she asked.

"Nothing, Mom."

"What do you mean 'nothing'? Your face is bloody."

"Just a fight."

"Otra fight? I thought we'd settled this. Why do you get into all these fights, Ray?"

"Don't know."

"That's not good enough," said Chelo. "This is the third time, and it looks like you got the worst of it." Chelo wiped her hands on her apron and pulled back two chairs at the kitchen table.

"Sit with me, Ray," she said. "Tell your old lady what's happening." She tore off a sheet of paper towel, folded it in half, and wet it under the tap.

"Hold your head up, so I can clean that nose," she said. Chelo wiped his chin, his cheeks, his downy mustache. Rolling a corner of the paper towel into a point, she cleaned out his bloody nostril. His eyelashes were so beautiful she wanted to weep. She could smell him. Sweat. Tres Flores hair tonic. "Boy," she whispered. "Ray, you gotta stop this fighting. You're not good at it, and they're going to ruin your movie star face." He smiled a bit.

"Are you gonna tell me what happened, or will I have to torture you?"

Raymundo exhaled. "Okay. I called Mateo Valenzuela a name, he called me a name, and it turned into a fight."

"Mateo. You need to avoid that one. I know that whole family. Bunch of thugs. Even the grandma is an old-school chola thug in that family." They both laughed heartily, and Raymundo relaxed.

"It's true," said Raymundo. "Their grandma is scary with those painted-on eyebrows, y todo."

"You never used to fight. What's up, Ray?"

"Nothing. Jus' people make me mad."

"What do they do?"

"Stupid shit. It irritates me."

"Like what? Are they picking on you because of your hair? Do they think you're a sissy?" Raymundo paused. She was right, but he couldn't have this discussion with her.

"No. Lots of people wear it long. All the stoners wear it long."

"But they're different. You're not a stoner. Or at least you better not be. Maybe if you cut it a little shorter."

"No. It's my style. I gotta go to the bathroom, okay?"

"Doesn't have to be a crew cut," said Chelo. "Just something shorter."

"Can I go, please?"

"Okay. But this is the last fight, Ray. Punto y final."

He stretched out across his bed, hands crossed behind his head. His hand wandered under his shirt to the tender triangle left by Mateo's shoe. He sighed, closed his eyes, and quickly factored in the variables necessary to forecast his future at San Benito Junior High. He tried to arrive at an encouraging scenario, but each time, his calculus failed. The whole school would soon know of him, and nothing could stop it. He had become a black hole. Everything in sight would hurtle through space in to collapse on him.

Raymundo heard a timid knock at his door.

"Who is it?" he asked.

"Me," said his little sister, Margie. She poked her round head in the doorway.

"Ray, wanna play Barbies with me?"

"Not today, Margie."

"How about hopscotch? Candy Land?"

"Not today."

"Please?"

"Margie, I'm thinking. Jus' close the door."

"How about if we play for only ten or seven minutes? Then you can think some more."

"Jus' gooooo. Go now. Go watch TV and close the door. I'm thinking."

"What are you thinking?"

"I'm thinking how I can go back to school" he said, sitting up. Margie stopped and studied his eye.

"You can go on the bus, like always," offered Margie.

"Go now, Margie. I promise we'll play Barbies tomorrow."

Reluctantly, she left. Raymundo lay on his side, face to the wall, hugging his pillow, and immediately fell asleep. He never felt Chelo take off his shoes and cover him. When she woke him for school fourteen hours later, he protested.

"Mom, I don't want to go on the school bus. Please let me sleep for a while more and start school late today. I don't feel good." Chelo patted his shoulder, nodded, and left him in bed. Almost three hours later, Raymundo rose and undressed, watching himself in the mirror. He had been appraising his classmates all semester and saw that some of them were becoming mannish. He wondered when he would graduate from this boyish androgyny that he rather liked but everyone else seemed to hate. Raymundo expertly picked himself apart: the skinny neck, uneven balls, narrow shoulders. He raked his fingers through his long hair and shook it out.

"At least I'm good from the neck up," he announced to his reflection. After a long, hot shower, the bruise on his eye seemed even more vivid. Going back to school felt stressful, but he'd already told his mother he was going. He put on his favorite jeans: snug from the knees up and spreading into magnificent bells at the bottom. In his mother's room, he sifted through her vanity for makeup and applied a bit to his bruise. It helped. He was ready to go. On his way out of his mother's bedroom, he saw it hanging on the door.

"Wow." He lifted it to the light.

"Beautiful." He ran it through his hands.

"Perfect. It's perfect." He had never before seen a belt formed of golden chain links.

The simple genius of it thrilled him. *A chain an' a belt at the same time*, he thought to himself. He wrapped it about his narrow waist twice, buckled it, and draped the ends down the front of his pants. "Time to go to school," he said to himself in the mirror.

* * *

Walking to school, Raymundo counted railroad ties and took pleasure in the clinking sound of the ends of the belt. Periodically, he looked down to admire the movement of it and shifted his hips wider with each step to increase the arc of the swing. The truck pulled up behind him so slowly he hardly noticed it.

"Hey, kid!" shouted someone.

Raymundo reined in his strut, tightened his body, and turned his head. It was a young guy, maybe twenty years old, in a blue Ford pickup with the words JV ROOFING on the door. Raymundo quickly assessed what he saw and did not recognize the man.

"You should get off those tracks, buddy," he said to Ray. "It's dangerous. I remember on Easter Sunday some guy got hit by a train on the tracks."

"I think he was a hobo," said Raymundo. "Probably drunk on the tracks."

"Still. Gotta be careful, yeah?" His voice was friendly. Raymundo relaxed, moved off the tracks, and continued walking on the gravel that lined the railroad.

"Where you walking to?"

"School," said Raymundo.

"You want a ride?" he asked.

"No thanks," said Raymundo. "I'll jus' walk." Raymundo noted his nice smile. He knew that he would save time if he accepted the ride, but he was not anxious to get to school. Still, the guy looked reassuring with his tidy mustache, blue button-up shirt, and baseball cap.

"I'm Lorenzo," said the driver, holding out his hand through the open window of the truck. Raymundo automatically walked toward him with his own hand outstretched.

"I'm Raymundo." They shook hands and Raymundo felt his hand swallowed up by Lorenzo's thick fingers. Raymundo loosened his grip, but Lorenzo held his hand for a few extra beats before letting go. Raymundo's heart began to pump harder.

"It looks like you're heading to San Benito," said Lorenzo. "You like that school?"

"It's okay."

"Looks like it's pretty rough there," he said, glancing at Raymundo's bruised face. Raymundo said nothing.

"My nephew goes there," said Lorenzo. "You know Joey Sandoval?"

"Yeah. I know him," responded Raymundo.

"Small world. You guys friends?"

"Not really."

"You want some Fritos?" asked Lorenzo, holding out an opened bag.

"No thanks. I just brushed my teeths."

"You got a girlfriend, Ray?" Raymundo cast his eyes down and studied the painted lettering on the door.

"No."

"C'mon, are you being shy? If you do, don't hold back."

"I'm not lucky with girls."

"Me neither," Lorenzo replied. Raymundo glanced at Lorenzo sideways and wondered how *he* could be unlucky.

"Well, you're good-looking, Raymundo. Girls will start coming to you soon enough." Lorenzo patted Raymundo's shoulder, and there his hand stayed.

"Is this okay?" asked Lorenzo.

"Yes, it's okay," said Raymundo. Before he could stop himself, Raymundo reached up and brushed his hand over Lorenzo's, grazing the fine hairs on his knuckles. Raymundo became self-conscious and quickly dropped his hand and shifted out of Lorenzo's reach. The brief moment of silence that followed was awkward, punctuated by a gawky exchange of smiles. Raymundo felt his heart working hard and his erection began to press against his jeans. He wanted to both stay and run away from this overwhelming scenario.

"I gotta get to school," said Raymundo in a quiet panic.

"Okay, no problem. I just thought you could use a ride."

"I feel like walking," said Raymundo. "I'll see you later, Lorenzo." Raymundo began to walk away when Lorenzo called out.

"Can I give you my number?"

"Is it the number painted on the door?"

"No, that's my work number," said Lorenzo, "I'll give you my home number." Lorenzo reached across the seat to the glove compartment. As he stretched, Lorenzo's T-shirt rode up, and Raymundo glimpsed the dark hairs on Lorenzo's pale belly. Lorenzo took out a business card and a pen, wrote his number on the back, and handed it to Raymundo.

"Ray, it was nice to meet you. You've got my number, so call if you feel like it. Any time."

"See you later," said Raymundo.

"I hope so," said Lorenzo.

By the time Raymundo arrived, students were transitioning from fifth to sixth period. As he walked to his locker, he felt eyes on his bruised face. Mateo and Joey swooped over to Raymundo as he crouched down to open his locker. Raymundo pretended not to see them and proceeded to enter the padlock combination.

"What the fuck is that fruit wearing now?" asked Joey.

"He's wearing his fuckin' disco belt, " said Mateo.

"Move it in, move it out, shove it in, round and about, disco lady!" sang Joey.

"We should hang you by that lady belt, Raygay," said Mateo. They laughed as Raymundo dug out his notebook, closed the locker, and stood.

"If you're not saying nothing," said Mateo, "that means you're admitting that you're a queer fag."

"If I say I'm not a fag, you won't believe me," said Raymundo. "So I'll say I am. Y que?"

"Hah, I knew it," crowed Mateo. "A fag! You got a boyfriend and everything, puto?"

"Maybe," responded Raymundo. The tart response caught them off guard.

"Excuse me," Raymundo said, slipping between Mateo and Joey. "I gotta go to woodshop." Raymundo tossed his hair, turned smartly on his heels, and crossed an unmarked border into a new country.

Raymundo the Fag

Raymundo the Fag's great gift and burden was to look any woman in the face and envision the perfect hairdo for her. The route to maximum beauty always seemed clear to him, a luminous path that glowed as if marked in reflective highway paint. When asked, he told his clients the truth and pointed the way to the via bella, but not everyone was ready to walk that narrow path. Sadly, they could not imagine the glories of what he saw for them, the haircut that soared beyond fashion and even taste to hover in the rarified realm of *eleganza*. None of this could they see on their march toward the unholy mirage of their preferred haircut. Raymundo always gave his clients what they asked for, but each time they declined his offer of *eleganza*, they unknowingly pricked his heart. Like all prophets, he suffered horribly.

For consolation, he cast himself back to his childhood Sunday school classes, where he once asked Sister Sarah: "Have you always been a nun?" When she began her reply by uttering, "Way back when I was a child," he was visibly shocked. It had not occurred to Raymundo that nuns were ever anything else. He had never seen a baby nun, of course, but like the proverbial baby pigeons that no one has ever seen, baby nuns had to exist somewhere, immaculately conceived and beatifically rolling Play-Doh nativity scenes at nun preschools. Sister Sarah smiled and said, "I felt my vocation early on." She read his confusion and continued. "My vocation was God talking to me and telling me to commit myself to service in the church. It's like a voice that helps me know what I'm supposed to do."

"Vocation" seemed to Raymundo a word of magic, enfolding destiny, passion, and work. Vocation became the grail that shimmered just beyond Raymundo's fingertips as he labored at Bebe's Beauty Box, the grande dame of Watsonville's beauty salons. As he went about his work, he wondered if mere haircutting could constitute so exalted a thing.

No one else doubted Raymundo's talents. He was barely twenty-two years old and less than two years out of beauty college, but he already had the biggest client base in the salon. He initially had only random walk-ins and a handful of old friends as clients, but their numbers swelled quickly. His regulars were unflagging in their loyalty and fervent in their evangelizing on his behalf. Such was the case with Cookie, a regular who waved at him through the window as she approached. Even before she crossed the threshold of Bebe's Beauty Box, he began appraising her. She was cute and plump in the way that captivated and wounded the migrant Mexican lettuce pickers who gathered about the Watsonville City Plaza to watch the girls go by on Thursday evenings when the Main Street shops had weekly sidewalk sales. Cookie's skin was a perfect, even brown, and she favored the severe chola makeup of the time, with dark lipstick, heavy eyeliner, and meticulously drawn eyebrows. Her face was forever girlish in its pleasant round-ness. He could also see that she had been faithful with her regimen of brushing and conditioning. The silken shifting of hair that animated her every step started a tickle in his belly. He could see the optimal Cookie cut, but alas, she held up a copy of *People* magazine. The cover featured the three pretty stars of *Charlie's Angels*, the wildly popular female detective show. The two brunette angels flanked the blonde angel. He braced himself, knowing what was coming next.

"Hey, Mundo," asked Cookie, "can you do me a cut like hers in the picture?"

"You mean the Farrah Fawcett cut?"

"Yeah. The Farrah. All feathered on the sides like that, but bigger."

"Hey, Cookie. This cut is nice, and it is so popular right now, but can I tell you about another cut that you might like?"

"No, homey. I don't want a Dorothy Hamill or whatever you're thinking."

"Who said anything about a Dorothy Hamill?" asked Ray. "That's too short for you. I want to recommend—"

"Don't. My mind is made up, and I want the Farrah."

"Okay, chica, the Farrah it is."

*   *   *

Cookie's scalp was marvelous, a dense forest of dark shafts. An amateur would have said she has straight black hair. But Raymundo perceived the deep brown and even auburn sub-strata of color. He could also see it was not completely straight. Instead it was weighted down by its own length. Two and a half inches off the ends would lessen the weight and acti-vate the latent waves and volume critical to the Farrah cut. Raymundo's days were often a succession of back-to-back appointments broken only by a rushed lunch break, so he worked on Cookie quickly. He pinned her up and trimmed section by section, gossiping a bit but mostly listening, to sweeten the tip. His hands and words were deft and light and soon she opened up.

"Manny keeps saying 'no more kids,' so I haven't told him yet that we got another mocoso on the way."

"He hasn't noticed yet?" asked Raymundo.

"I'm a fatty, so when I put on fifteen pounds, bonehead Manny doesn't even notice. It's a good thing he's dumb, aye."

"He might be slow," said Raymundo. "But eventually he'll find out. Then what?"

"Then he shits a brick when I tell him. Oh well, screw him. After six years together, he should know I can't always remember the pill, so he needs to use protection too. Besides, with two girls, I'm ready to try for a boy. He'll be into it if it's finally a boy. That's how guys are. He'll get completely culeco, like a chicken with her eggs. And if he doesn't like it, tough titty."

Raymundo worked the finish obsessively, snipping at the tips, blowing out the fullness, balancing the symmetry, and feathering the bangs to capacity. Finally, his scissors went quiet.

"Close your eyes, chica," he warned. He brushed the clippings from her forehead and neck, and pulled off the drape with a magician's flourish.

"Mirror, mirror on the wall, who's the Farrah of them all?" he asked. Cookie giggled as he swiveled her chair toward the mirror.

"Ta daaah! Whaddya think, Cookie?" Her eyes watered over. She looked upset. His abdominal muscles clenched. Her lips parted, and she said nothing. Finally, she spoke. "Iss beautiful, Mundo. Perfect."

He was a junkie for this moment.

Cookie left him a tip of three quarters wrapped in two sweaty dollars she'd been holding in her hand. This represented the better part of an hour of scooping ice cream at Thrifty.

"Thanks, corazón," said Raymundo. "I'll see you later."

"Definitely see you later. Thanks so much for the cut, Mundo. I love it, love it, love it." Sashaying to her car, Cookie checked herself in the salon window. Raymundo's coworker

Olga, on her way back from lunch, crossed paths with Cookie and fussed over the new haircut. Cookie drove away with a vigorous wave goodbye, and Olga entered the salon.

"Another happy customer," said Olga with a roll of her eyes.

"Yeah," he said. "That cut looks like it fell on her head from another planet, but what the hell? I styled it up the yin-yang and she's happy. That's all we can do, sister."

"Ray, I've known Cookie since we were kids, and let me tell you she is a tough customer in every way. She's got a mean mouth and strong opinions about beauty. The first time I saw Cookie coming toward the salon, I thought, Chingue su madre, and I hid in the back because I didn't want to be her hairdresser. If you can keep that loca happy, that shows that you are really good at hair."

"So are you, Olga."

"Yeah, I'm good at it, but you're really good. You ever think of getting a chair someplace bigger, like San Francisco?"

"Nope," said Raymundo. "I don't like big cities. I mean, I like going up there clubbing once in a while, but every time I go, I spend half my time trying to find a parking spot. Besides, there's probably a million stylists up there. It's like the elephant graveyard in the old Tarzan movies. The hair burners migrate there from all over the country. They can't help it. Animal instinct."

"Yeah, but you can build up clients."

"I've got lots of clients here in Watsonville. Business is good, Olga. I'm not saying that's the same as getting a degree and some big-deal career, but I'm not complaining. It's real beautiful out here. The orchards, the ocean, the weather. I am a flor silvestre, Olga. I belong in the country. Wildflower power!"

"Well then how about a bigger town, like Salinas?" said Olga. "That's country too."

"Chica, it's taken this town twenty-five years to get used to me, but they finally have. I'm the town fruit. Not the best job in the world, but it's mine and I paid for it big-time. Half the culeros in this town have harassed or beat me, when they weren't trying to get into my pants. But I'm still here and taking their money to make their wives and girlfriends look foxy. That's home, Olga. I'm not going nowhere. Besides, what would I do without my regulars?" he asked as he gestured to the door.

As if on cue, the bells on the door jingled as Mrs. Katarina Kusanovich entered. Special K, as he called her, pulled in every Friday at exactly 1:00 p.m. Old-school to her bones, she favored gloves for her outings and wore adorable couture magically ferreted out of thrift stores and garage sales in the tonier neighborhoods of Monterey and Carmel. That day she sported a houndstooth Chanel number from the midsixties. The hemline was unfashionably high and probably not age appropriate, but Katarina was devoted to full-spectrum accessorizing, from earrings to autos, and felt convinced the Chanel suit went perfectly with her immaculate 1956 Nash Rambler.

"Special K! How are you?"

"I'm a mess, Rayboy. Save me."

"How can you say that? You're the most put-together woman since Jackie O."

"Right after they shot Kennedy, maybe."

"I'm serious, your outfit is super pre-retro, very chic."

"I've had this one forever. Have I told you about the fateful Saturday I found this?"

"Yes, and if you repeat that story one more time, you're walking out with a mohawk. Now sit yourself down and let me work my magic."

If Special K had been a man, she would not have enough hair to do a convincing combover. Hers was a sobering head. Each silver strand seemed forlorn, wondering where everyone had gone. Nevertheless, she insisted on an outdated bouffant circa the Lady Bird Johnson administration. The construction of Special K's signature hairdo was exceedingly tricky. It was an airy cathedral of a cut based on an architecture of Aqua Net and prayer. Raymundo blew and teased and teased some more, and slowly it rose. He shifted what he could to the front and spread it as far as it would go in the back: a cotton candy crisscross that looked miraculously full. Soon, no further amplification was possible.

"It's done."

"Let's see it."

"It's so good I can't stand it."

"Let's see already!" she said.

"Oh you wicked, wicked sorceress. The paparazzi will shit little green apples when they see this bouffant."

Raymundo spun her chair toward the mirror. Special K gazed at herself square on. She arched one eyebrow and spoke directly to Raymundo's reflection.

"If you ever leave this town, Rayboy, I'm following you."

The special phone call followed two hours after Katarina and her Rambler had pulled away. Throughout the busy day, Raymundo had not taken any phone calls. In the middle of a rinse, he saw Bebe, the salon proprietor, stretching the telephone curly cord across the width of the shop to pass him the receiver.

"Oye, Ray," said Bebe. "It's someone from Eastlake Memorial Chapel. He called while you were doing Katarina's hair, so I asked him to call back. Raymundo excused himself from his client, wiped his hands, and lifted the receiver to his ear. A soft, evenly modulated voice addressed him.

"Hello, sir. I'm Rodney, calling from Eastlake Memorial Chapel. So sorry to bother you today, but we have a situation with one of our clients and you come highly recommended as someone with the skills to help us with our situation."

Raymundo pressed the phone harder against his ear to better hear the soft utterings.

"What can I help you with?" asked Raymundo.

"Well, sir, it seems that sadly we have a homicide victim out here in Hollister. Point-blank gunshot."

"Oh my goodness."

"Yes, he was very unfortunate and this is a tragic loss to his family. When they shot him, the bullet left a hole toward the back of the left side of his head. Of course, we would never lay him out for viewing with all that missing tissue, so we got a wig for him. The deceased's wife saw it, and she was not satisfied. She said it wasn't him because the hair was wrong. We tried to restyle the wig, but nothing we did satisfied her, and finally she got agitated and said we could no longer touch his hair, well, his wig. She has asked that we bring you to work on the wig." Raymundo took a moment to take in what Rodney was saying.

"Are you serious?"

"Yes, sir," said Rodney. "I realize this is probably unusual, but she insisted that you were the only one who could help. Can you work with us? It would mean a lot to her."

"Who is this woman?"

"Rosie Pardo Archebeque."

"Rosie Archebeque? Thin, short, hazel eyes?"

"Yes."

"I know Rosie from back in high school. Years ago, I used to cut her hair regularly, then she suddenly stopped coming. I think she moved to Gilroy or something. I didn't know she'd married one of the Pardos. I thought she didn't like those Pardo boys. That's beside the point, though. Tell me, what is the dead man's name?"

"Mauricio."

"Oh jeez. I knew all those Pardos, but I never knew their real names. Only the nicknames. Either way, I'll help. Rosie has always been real nice."

"Wonderful. I think it would be a great comfort to her. You can bill us whatever is necessary. When might you be able to swing by?"

"The only time I really have is early tomorrow before work," said Raymundo. "How about seven thirty a.m.?"

"Great. Thank you. That is just fantastic, sir. We're at 237 Junipero Serra Street in Hollister. Do you know Bingo Burgers?"

"Of course. Everyone knows Bingo Burgers," said Raymundo.

"We're two buildings down from Bingo Burgers, in the red brick building. We'll see you tomorrow."

Raymundo brooded through the rest of the day. His small talk contracted, and he offered only noncommittal vocalizations to the stream of chatter from his clients. In contrast, Olga was noticeably starstruck by the Eastlake Memorial Chapel call. As she swept up after a client, she fussed over the call.

"Oh my God, Ray," said Olga, "You're famous. They called you to do this special job all the way from over there."

"Ay, Olga, Hollister is about twenty minutes away."

"Doesn't matter. They knew about your work and they called for you."

"It's a haircut. No big deal."

"Yes it is. They need you. It's a tragedy, it's special. Hey, do they pay good?"

"Olga! He's dead, remember?"

"Well, there you go. He won't be tipping, so you need to charge them good up front. For gasoline y todo."

"Yes, Mrs. Scrooge."

"They got equipment for you?"

"Probably not. Guess I'll take my big ol' Gucci emergency care hair burner purse like the doctor on *Little House on the Prairie*." At his car trunk, Raymundo rooted through the clothing, tools, and magazines until he excavated his gym bag and emptied it out. Plucking items from his workstation, he packed everything he might need into the bag and headed home for an early night in.

The clock buzzed promptly at six in the morning. Raymundo ate some cold cereal, showered, shaved, and selected a black knit shirt for the day. Unaccustomed to driving at this hour, he was surprised at the stream of early Saturday farmworker traffic on Route 152. Still, he made it to Hollister in a half hour and knocked at Eastlake Memorial Chapel. The oak door swung open and a broad slab of a man filled the doorframe.

"Hi. I'm Ray and I'm here to do a job for Rodney."

"That would be me." As they shook hands, Raymundo registered the firm, restrained pressure of Rodney's beefy hands.

"You didn't sound like a linebacker on the phone, Rodney. I was expecting more of a five-foot-four professor kind of guy."

"We morticians talk small. Please come in, Raymundo, and I'll get you set up." Rodney led him through the office and down the stairs, talking as they descended.

"We have reference photos for you to work from and a new wig. The original wig is . . . no longer with us."

"Gone home to Jesus?"

"Let's just say it's in a better place."

Downstairs, the fluorescent mundanity of the workroom was almost disappointing to Raymundo. Shelves of cleaning supplies, file cabinets, wicker flower stands. Only the stainless steel worktables and gurneys gave away the purpose of the place. Rodney placed his right hand on Ray's shoulder and with his free hand, he offered an orientation.

"You can work at this counter. These are the hot and cold water taps, be careful because the hot water is extremely hot. Disinfectant and gloves are right here on the shelf. Trash cans are over there. Bathroom is on the right by the service elevator and that's my desk over there, so holler if you need anything. And most critically, the coffee machine is back near the corner." Rodney walked to a file cabinet, reached into the top drawer, and produced a business envelope.

"Here are the reference photos." Raymundo opened the folder and began studying the small stack of photos. The first photo had the caption of "Birthday, 1979," written in the corner. In the photo, a young man with a maniacal grin sat behind an adorably lopsided homemade cake. With a kitchen knife, he feigned a stabbing motion toward the frosted heart of it. The numeric candles read "24." So handsome. Movie star teeth. Raymundo sucked air and went still.

"Everything okay?" asked Rodney.

"I knew him. He was called Shy Boy. I did my first Holy Communion with him," said Raymundo.

"I'm sorry you lost a friend today, Raymundo. These small towns. Everyone's connected. Were you pretty close to him?"

"No. Heck, I didn't even know his real name was Mauricio. We took catechism together for a few weeks and did our Communion. Once, he and his friends bullied me for a bit. Not fun, but then he disappeared from school."

"Oh. I'm sorry that happened."

Raymundo studied the second picture. Shy Boy and two standard-issue cholo homeboys with sharply creased T-shirts and pants, web belts, and all the shiny brilliantine their hair could hold. Dimples and teeth. Arms draped across each other's shoulders. Affectionate. Fraternal. Their hands are busy, forming gang glyphs: finger pistols, tripods, and hooks.

"Looks like maybe Shy Boy fell in with a rough crowd," said Rodney.

"Shy Boy was the rough crowd," said Raymundo.

"His wife, Rosie, is a tough one too," said Rodney. "She kept complaining about why those so-called machos couldn't just beat each other up like real men instead of using guns."

"That sounds like Rosie, all right."

"Here's the new wig for you to style," said Rodney. "You can work straight from the photos, we can pull him out of the cooler, or you can see him in the cooler. Whatever you like. The right side of his head is intact, and you can still see his hair."

"I'll have a look at him in the cooler," said Raymundo. They entered the cooler. Three coffins on wheeled trolleys were lined up inside.

"You've got a full house here, Rodney. You should install parking meters."

"Two were from a traffic accident. Siblings, eighteen and fourteen."

"Oh no. I'm sorry. That was dumb of me to say that. I guess this is not a good place for joking."

"Actually, it's the best place. Long as there's no family around." Rodney pulled one of the trolleys out of the cooler and opened the top half of the coffin lid.

"Here's Mauricio. I'll be right outside. When you've finished looking him over, let me know, and I'll close it up again." Rodney stepped out of the cooler and the wide door closed behind him with a click.

"Alone at last," said Raymundo to Shy Boy. He gazed at the face, and noted it looked much as it had in high school. A wave of sadness moved through Raymundo as he studied Shy Boy's young face. Rodney had talent. From the right side, the face seemed a bit waxy but almost normal. He imagined Rodney's hands smoothing the shock and misery from Shy Boy's face, dusting a bit of counterfeit life onto the cheeks, and tying the half-Windsor knot at his throat.

Shy Boy's hair felt alive. Raymundo rubbed it between his fingers. It felt like it was on the thicker end of fine but not quite medium weight. A bit of natural wave. Simple part with feathers to the left and right. Why had it been so difficult to approximate this? As he studied, Raymundo realized it was the same hairstyle Shy Boy had used back in high school. He remembered the way Shy Boy and his friends once accosted him on his walk home from school. They made kissy sounds when he passed. They branded him with the usual array of sissified labels. Raymundo remembered that it was probably Shy Boy that first called him Raygay, the one name that stuck. He remembered realizing that Shy Boy had not been to school in weeks and feeling relief to have one less person around to hassle him, even if the others were ready to pick up where Shy Boy had left off.

Raymundo examined the broken side of Shy Boy's head. The top of the ear was gone. The wig could cover that. He ran his hand along the edge of the gaping head wound. At the lip of the crater, he felt the skin on the scalp turn up slightly. He craned and looked. Where there was enough tissue, the site was stitched up. The rest of it was open.

"Ooh, Shy Boy. I'm so sorry. They really got you." Raymundo pondered the fluids and signals coursing through his own brain. He wondered if this bit of plumbing and hardware was really all there was to a person. A second, greater wave of sadness suffused him. He placed his hand over Shy Boy's heart and spoke. "About the Raygay thing, that was messed up but no hard feelings. In honor of your wife, Rosie, I'll make you foxy again."

When he held the wig that Eastlake Memorial Chapel had provided, Raymundo immediately felt the problem. He turned it inside out and checked the label. He called out to Rodney, who rejoined him in the cooler.

"Rodney," said Raymundo, "I think I know why you had so much trouble satisfying Rosie. This is a human hair wig. They're usually made with Chinese people's hair. Beautiful product, very thick and dark. But that's the problem. It's too thick to look like Shy Boy's hair. Most people wouldn't notice the difference, but of course Rosie isn't 'most people.' She's his wife."

"What should we do?" asked Rodney.

"I have a wig in the trunk of my car," offered Raymundo. "And I think I can cut it down to get a good match." Rodney exhaled and smiled.

"That sounds perfect. If you have a more appropriate wig, that would be tremendous. We'll cover that cost, of course."

At his car trunk, Raymundo dug out his purple overnight bag. The Wonder Woman costume inside had been a hit at the Halloween street party in San Francisco's gay quarter. Lynda Carter's *Wonder Woman* was big that year, so he saw lots of knobby-kneed brethren ranging about on spike-heeled red boots. Nevertheless, he felt that with his elegant legs and superior wig, he was one of the more wondrous of the Wonder Women. Every few steps, a stranger would grab his mighty Amazonian breasts. Drunken frat boys pretended to nurse from him on either side as he threw his head back in mock ecstasy. More modest folk begged to be lassoed for a snapshot. He pulled back the bobby pins to detach the golden headband from the wig and then shook it out.

"Not too bad, my pretty," he said to the wig. "Come with me. We have a mission." Raymundo headed back down the stairs into the chapel basement. Rodney was on the phone, so Raymundo let him know everything was under control by shaking the wig at him. Rodney gave a thumbs-up and smiled. Raymundo went right to work, shampooing the wig and brushing out the snarls. Rodney finished his phone call and came over for a closer look.

"Wow. You had the right wig in your car trunk. I'm impressed. No wonder Rosie insisted on you, Ray. You don't mind if I call you Ray?"

"No Rod, I don't mind at all," responded Raymundo. They both smiled and Raymundo went back to work on the wig. He pinned it to a Styrofoam wig stand and trimmed it down to pageboy length and parted it clean down the center.

Sculpting down the sides, he created a soft taper that he estimated would conform to the shape of Shy Boy's head. He studied the birthday snapshot again. With a brush and a hot iron set to low, he replicated the graceful sweep of his feathers. Putting down everything, he stepped back and appraised his progress, moving his eyes between wig and photo. He fussed with the length of the sideburn and squared the corners of the neckline. He rose and stalked the wig from all sides and at various angles.

"It's looking good, Ray," said Rodney from his desk. "Is it done?"

"I don't know. I'll have to see it on him. Rod, can I go ahead and try it on him?"

"Yes, Ray, no problem."

Raymundo entered the cooler, carefully slipped the wig onto Shy Boy's head, and pushed the stray locks under the edge of the wig.

"We're so close now," Raymundo said to Shy Boy. "Just a few adjustments, and we're good."

He pinned the wig back on the wig stand and trimmed back the crown by a quarter of an inch. Then he sprayed it with Aqua Net once, twice, and a third time, letting it dry between coats. As he studied the extravagant feathering and ambitious upward poof of it all, it began to look ridiculous on the long-necked wig stand. Doubt blossomed in Ray's chest. Back in the cooler, he placed the wig back on Shy Boy. Sweet Jesus. It was perfect. He grazed it with the back of his hand and thought of a geisha he once saw in *National Geographic*. Her wig was a lacquered, sculptural form of improbable, sweeps and volumes, yet it seemed inevitably perfect on her head. Was it just a happy accident of fashion that this wig, cut in the popular style of the day also happened to be inevitably perfect for Shy Boy? All of this was beyond knowing, but as he assessed his handiwork with swelling pride, the haircut looked to Raymundo like the raven glory that God himself would want to see crowning the head of Mauricio "Shy Boy" Pardo.

Ofelia's Last Ride

Last September, our radiator exploded while we drove past Palm Desert on our way to Mexico. When Pa opened up the hood of our poor Impala station wagon, a cloud of smoke and steam flew up like a pissed-off ghost. Pa burned his hand trying to fix the broken hoses and shouted at the radiator. It only took about twenty minutes, but while we were waiting, the inside of the car got so hot we had to step outside into the desert sun to cool off. This year, we're going back, but we're driving to my Nana Leti's at night, so we won't be in the desert when the sun is out. It takes about eleven hours to drive there, so my ma and pa take turns driving. Ma made fresh tortillas and rolled up a bunch of burritos in 'luminum foil for the trip, because we only stop to get gas or pee.

I don't like fifth grade, and I'm glad this trip will get me out of school for a week. When I told my new teacher, Miss MacDoogal, that I was going away for a week, she gave me a funny look. I don't think she liked the idea. I told her a big, fat lie and said my grandpa had died and we had to go to Mexico. She was cool after that. I don't always like being in Ma and Pa's barrio in Mexicali, but I like getting there. Pa never drinks when we make this drive. He and Ma are usually in a good mood, because they're going to see family and friends, and they can be the adults, doing whatever they need to do in Spanish instead of asking us to translate into English for them. It's dark, so I can't read while we ride. Instead, we listen to the radio or count Volkswagen Beetles. When I feel sleepy, I lie down in the back of the station wagon under my blanket and watch the stars pass by the window. Around Mecca, it gets exciting because we start to hear Radio Variedades, the big radio station in Mexicali. The station plays everything: cumbias, rancheras, boleros. They talk about the weather and tell jokes. The DJ makes his words into a big deal. He doesn't say "rodeo" like everyone else. He says "rrrrrrrrrooooooodeooooo." When he gives the news, he talks about stuff in Mexico I don't understand. When he mentions President Carter, he pronounces the name "Yeemy Cahrter."

When we get to El Centro, Ma makes sure everyone is awake. We're very close to la linea, the border. There is a ghost that people see hitchhiking on the side of the highway at night. If you give her a ride, she'll get in and disappear. If you don't, she'll sit on the hood of your car and try to make you crash.

"Should we pick her up if we see her?" asks Pa.

"No, that's a bad idea," I say. "We should drive away fast."

"Yes, we should pick her up," says Sylvie. "I want to see her up close. Besides, we have lots of room in this big boat."

"Maybe she wants a burrito," says Ma.

"Maybe she wants our souls," says Pa. We start laughing, but I'm kind of nervous as we drive through El Centro. The sun is coming out as we get near Calexico. It's funny, those two cities on the border have crisscrossed names. Calexico in the California side. Mexicali in the Mexico side. The two cities kiss each other through the big border fence. Before we cross la linea, Ma stops driving and Pa takes the wheel because the driving in Mexicali is cuckoo for Cocoa Puffs. At the border, the guard waves us right in, and we wave back at him as we pass. As soon as we cross, everything changes. It is early in the morning, but there are hundreds of people and hundreds of cars lined up to cross into Calexico. I see men, women, and even little kids walking around selling things on the road. Hot coffee, bottles of water, sombreros, and sodas. Gum and candies. Tacos. Newspapers. Everything is busy and moving. Pa drives us past the border streets, and we head to the Colonia Baja California neighborhood. Sometimes the road is cement, sometimes it's dirt. Driving to Nana Leti's house, I recognize a few places. Las Rosas tortilla factory and bakery, the Nuestra Señora del Perpetuo Socorro church, the little dirt soccer field. When we arrive, Ma says a prayer and thanks the Virgin of Guadalupe that we are safe. We get out of the station wagon and Pa shouts from outside of my nana's iron gate.

"Madre mia, please let us in!" he says. My Nana Leti comes out. Her hands are wet from washing dishes, and she dries them off on her apron. Her hair is pulled back in a braid, and she is wearing a blue dress and blue plastic sandals. I wave at her through the gate, and even before she unlocks it, she is crying. Pa hugs her hard, and he cries too.

"Doña Leti, you look so good," says my ma when they hug.

"Hola, Esperanza," says Abuela to my ma. "Just look how pretty you are with those green cat eyes."

"Hola, mijo," she says to me. I hug her and she looks at me from my sneakers to my hair. "Dios mio, but you're getting so big and chubby like me. You're part of the family for sure!"

Normally, I don't like it when people tell me I'm fat, but she's my abuela, and she's not being mean about it, and I better get used to it, because here in the barrio everybody and their dog are going to remind me I'm fat. People who don't even know me call me Gordo. Three of my tios and tias step out, hug everyone, and help us unload our blankets and boxes, and we put everything in the little adobe bedroom the four of us are going to share. Ma and Pa will sleep on the big bed under the supermarket calendar with the picture of Jesus Christ with a burning heart. Sylvie will sleep in the tiny bed under the sad clown painting, and I'll sleep on the floor on a stack of blankets. I don't care if I sleep on the floor, because I'm tired. When Ma asks if I want to take a siesta, I say yes. The three of them leave me alone in the room, and I fall asleep right away.

* * *

When I wake up, I'm a little confused because nothing looks familiar. Then I remember we're in Mexicali. I can hear Grandma's doves in the backyard. She keeps them in a little wooden cage that hangs from the twisty pepper tree. I like putting my hand in the cage and feeding them. I can smell smoke everywhere, because some people in the barrio don't have stoves, so they use firewood to cook. I step outside, and Ma is sitting in the shade in front of the iron fence. I sit down in the chair next to her.

"Where's Pa?" I ask.

"You know where he is," says Ma. Dang. Pa is already out drinking with his friends. "And where's Sylvie?" I ask.

"She is out with your Tia Laura, getting groceries," says Ma. We sit together in the shade. Old friends and neighbors keep passing by and saying hi to Ma. She looks happy to be here, even if Pa is out drinking.

Coming down the block, we see Flaco. His bony grasshopper knees move up and down as he bikes to us. Flaco waves at Doña Sara, who is hosing down the street in front of her house to keep the dust down. Flaco nods to Don Fosforo, who has a big mob of kids waiting for a raspado. He is shaving ice so hard you can see the little chunks of it jumping up and sticking to his arm. From here, I can see the bottles of raspado flavors: yellow is mango, red is strawberry, and green is lime. Brown is tamarindo, the best of all the flavors. It makes my mouth all watery just thinking about it.

Near the corner, Flaco shouts, "Ese mi, Negro!" Negro looks up at him and smiles. I can see his perfect white teeth. I think Negro is about thirteen years old, but he's been shining shoes on that hot corner since forever and he's burned to the color of his shoe polish, even the part of his arms under the sleeve. That's why he's called Negro, and after a while in the barrio, your nickname takes over, and most people can't even remember your real name anymore.

Flaco stops and walks his bike to us at the fence, and he keeps saying: "Big news, big news, big news." If he wasn't so skinny, they'd probably call him El Periodico because he always has the news. Of course we want to know, so Ma asks him: "What's the big news today, mijo?"

"Big news from Palma Street," he says, and his eyes get big. "It's about Doña Ofelia."

"Is she sick?" asks Ma.

"No. Not anymore. The news is that Doña Ofelia is dead." Ma is quiet, then Flaco says, "Pati the Mouth says they found Doña Ofelia dead in bed, with beer bottles everywhere. Yesterday she served dinner right at six like always, then she went to lie down. She doesn't do that usually, so later Roberto the Sasquatch went to check on her and found her dead. The wake is tomorrow from four p.m. on their porch and the burial will happen the day after at noon. They asked me to tell the news to Doña Leti, and you're invited too, Doña Esperanza. You can come too, Gordo."

I never saw a dead person in person, so I ask, "Ma, can I go with you to see her?"

"Mijo, why do you want to go? You'll just get scared and have nightmares." She's probably right, but I want to go see a dead body. Besides, I hate it when Ma goes away. There is some mean people on this street. They call me all the fat names they can think of and then invent brand-new ones to show how mean they are. The boys here are pretty rough too. One kid from around the corner once threw a big rock at my forehead just because. My forehead got cut, but thank God my brains stayed in. I was littler then, so my pa grabbed that kid by the hair and dragged him to his house, where his own dad smacked him till his nose bled. My pa is a bad mama jamma. Most of the boys are afraid to hit me now, but they still make fun of my Spanish and ask how come I'm always with my ma, and do I do the dishes because I want to be a girl. I don't know why it's such a big deal to help. Even my Nana Leti asked why I like to work in the kitchen. I was glad when Ma said she loves it because I'm her best helper. Yeah, it'd be way better going to see a dead lady than staying here.

"Can I go, Ma?" I ask again. Finally, Ma says I can go, but if I get scared, it's not her fault.

The next morning, I wash my face and fix my hair with Tres Flores oil the way Pa taught me. My hair gets shiny like Superboy's. I feel like maybe I'm going to look super sharp in my button shirt, and I'm ready to see my first-ever dead body. Ma tried to wake up Pa and get him to get ready for the funeral, but he said his hangover was going to kill him and his head hurt and he would just go to the burial tomorrow instead. Sylvie said she doesn't want to see a dead body, so she is staying home. In the kitchen, Ma is cutting limes and cilantro to go with the big pot of pozole she made for Ofelia's wake. We say goodbye to Sylvie and begin walking to Ofelia's. We don't even get past two houses when Flora calls to Ma.

"ESPERAAAAANZA!" Oof. Flora's voice reminds me of those big ol' parrots they tell you not to pet in the pet shops.

"Esperanza, did you hear the news about Doña Ofelia?"

"Yes, I heard she left in her sleep two nights ago."

"Pobrecita. Oh well, at least she's not suffering anymore, may she rest in peace." Flora is pretty full of shit because Doña Ofelia never suffered. Every time I saw her, she was mostly pretty drunk and always laughing, with her big old mouth open and full of gold like when you see the inside of the Vatican for Christmas Mass on TV. She really doesn't have to rest in peace now, because that's all she did when she was alive. All day long she'd sit on the porch under the mesquite with an ice bucket of Tecates. The big ones. She had a console stereo on the porch. One of the legs was missing, so she used two bricks and a Bible, I swear to God, A BIBLE, to hold it up. She'd sit and jam to the oldest Mexican songs in the world and talk to anyone on the street: her neighbors, little kids, and even men she didn't know.

I'd be kind of embarrassed if she was my mom, but those ugly Sasquatch sons of hers must've liked Doña Ofelia all right, because everyone knows that at the end of each week, they gave her their entire melon-picker paychecks, and she'd put them together and give them back some allowance. They're like big kids, except they use their allowances on beer, girls, and cars instead of candy. When they bought the blue Firebird with the T-roof and the custom van with the little round windows on the sides at the same time, everyone started saying the brothers were sneaking marijuana across the border into Calexico. Sylvie said that people were saying that Doña Ofelia was sleeping on a mattress full of drug money and betting thousands of dollars at the wrestling matches. She was even buying gold rings and watches for El Puma. I know for a fact that El Puma, a champion wrestler, would never let her or nobody look at his face under the mask, so if she never saw his face, she must have fallen in love with the way he looks in those little black underwears and boots, which I don't blame her for, cuz he gots all kinds of muscles on his arms and chest and even his caboose looks hard, like two turtles taking a nap. Personally, it is my opinion that I think he looks good. Even my pa, who loves to make fun of everybody and their dog, shoes, and haircuts, says El Puma looks good.

Ma and I keep walking, and when we get near the corner, Negro waves and talks to us.

"Hola, Señora Esperanza. You want me to give Gordo a shine?" Ma looks down at my shoes. I feel embarrassed that he saw they are all scratchy and dusty, but she's not sure about getting a shine.

"Seño," he says. "If you're going to Doña Ofelia's, his shoes should look nice. Gotta look nice if you're going to pay respects, don't you think, seño?" She touches the side of her neck with her handkerchief.

"All right, mijo, but quickly okay? It's hot out here."
Negro tells me to put my foot up on his shoeshine box while
he kneels in the dirt. He begins the shine and his hands
just *go*. Voosh! Voosh! Voosh! He takes the dust off with his
brush. He opens the wax and smears it on. He tells me how
good it's gonna look and smiles. He rubs it in and pulls out
the cleaning rag, and he snaps it so pretty and fast. Pah! Pah!
Pah! And it's this dance with dirty hands and the dirty rag.
Pah! Pah! Pah! And his shoulders and muscles move under
his shirt with a wet spot on the back and I can't stop looking
at how beautiful he makes a stupid shoeshine. Ptoo! He spits
on my shoe and it gets even shinier and he tells me I look
good and the girls are gonna love me in those shoes and I
smile, cuz I'm excited that he said that, even though I don't
like girls yet. One more time with the brush and then BOOM,
the shoes look like they're fresh from the store window. He's
done and he smiles.

He reaches up for his money, and through the hole of
his sleeve I can see little black hairs in his underarm. When I
see this, I get this embarrassed feeling, like I saw him naked,
and then I feel super sorry that he's so nice but he's stuck on
this corner where the sun is going to cook him into a raisin
and he'll still be poor. Ma pays him and then I put my hand
into my pocket and all I have is American money, so I give
him my shiny fifty-cents coin. Negro looks at the coin and he
SMILES like it's Christmas. I smile at him too. His eyes are
color cafe with no milk.

"Thank you, seño," he says to Ma.

"Thank you, Isidro."

Isidro. Negro's real name is Isidro.

At Doña Ofelia's house, it is crowded. I see Nana Leti and my tias there already. They helped set everything up. Doña Ofelia's family is all over the place. There are even kids up in the tree branches, looking over everything like little monkeys with wild hair sticking up. When I see all the new people I don't know, I get shy. I wish I'd stayed home like Sylvie, reading my tia's Spanish comics or something. But it's too late, and now I gotta stay no matter what dumb things people say to me. Near the front gate, Doña Ofelia's sons, the two Sasquatches, are lined up and shaking people's hands and sometimes hugging people. I don't like being called names, and I know it's kind of mean to call them Sasquatches, but it's true that they look like that. They're tall and big, with really big heads and bushy hair, and once the Mexicali TV station started showing *El Hombre Bionico* with Lee Majors fighting the Sasquatch, well that's what everyone called them. Heck, even the three sisters are Sasquatch-sized in this family.

When Ma shakes hands with Roberto, the oldest Sasquatch brother, her hand looks like a pink baby hand.

"Ay, Roberto," she says. "Your poor madre's gone."

"Yeah," he says.

"I'm sorry, Roberto. The only good thing is that she didn't suffer. She went home in her sleep."

"True," says Roberto, looking at the ground.

I also shake their hands. Tavo, the number two Sasquatch, asks, "Are you Esperanza's little boy?"

"Yeah."

"Caramba, mi niño. You've grown!" He looks me up and down. "And look how fat you've gotten." He grabs my stomach and says real loud to Roberto: "How many pounds of chicharrónes do you think we could get off this one?"

"Awww, Gordo is just full of life," says Roberto. "He looks good, pretty like a pink piglet, not like those black bony monkey boys of yours. This is a healthy boy. Señora Esperanza!" he shouts to Ma. "What have you been feeding this boy? You hoping to sell him off by the pound?" He pinches my cheeks and everyone looks at me and laughs. Ma smiles and disappears into the house to join in the rosary. I pull my face away, and Roberto lets go of my cheeks. My face feels hot and my cheeks kind of hurt, but I like that he said I'm pretty, and then I don't like it because boys are supposed to be handsome not pretty. Then I really don't like it because he said I was like a piglet. A piglet! My God, people in Mexico will say anything.

I move through the crowd of people to see Doña Ofelia. Her coffin is a dusty-pink color. That's a good lady color. They put the coffin on the kitchen table, under the porch. When I get closer, I can smell her flowers, then I see her face. Her face looks more puffier than usual, and she normally wears more makeup than she has on now. Is that how it is with dead bodies? Are they all familiar but different? I reach out and touch my first dead hand and it feels almost normal but a little cool and hard, like a muscle. It's weird, because I'm touching a dead hand, and all around me the people are all talking, eating, and drinking like it was a picnic. Under her back, they put this big pink satin pillow. It is kind of creepy, because the way she's sitting up, it looks like she's trying to get out of the coffin. I'm glad it's not dark and there are lots of people around.

The bottom half of the coffin is closed and covered with all kinds of chrysanthemums and palm leaves. I know chrysanthemums because my pa used to work at Monterey Nurseries back in Watsonville, and he always brung chrysanthemums home. Even though chrysanthemums leave the water smelling like caca, they are very beautiful, especially the ones that are red on the top and gold underneath. All around the coffin they have flowers. They have red carnations that spell "madre," white gladiolus, roses with baby's breath, and, believe it or not, some Scrooge actually brought an empty mayonnaise jar full of pink and white oleander off some bush. They tried to make it all special and shit by wrapping 'luminum foil around the jar, but it didn't look too good.

The moms brung all kinds of food. The three Sasquatch sisters are busy behind the food table, serving everyone, shaking hands. There are beans, arroz, chili con carne, ma's pozole, stuff to make tortas, Peñafiel sodas, hot coffee and a big hill of pan dulce. This funeral is boss, man!

I go to the table, get a nice chocolate concha, and find a quiet corner to eat. I look around at everyone, and I notice no one is crying. The Sasquatches stand there all serious and shake hands and hug. Once people go past them, they turn around and drink from their beers until the next person arrives. Some of the family and neighbors standing next to the coffin don't even *pretend* to be upset. They look at her like they're at Safeway looking at pork chops or potatoes.

Before anybody tells me to go play with the little Sasquatch kids, I look for Ma inside the house. It's dark and empty in the first room, and I follow the sound of praying. I see her and a bunch of women and a few old guys kneeling for the rosary. The curtains are shut tight, but there are lots of candles. It is really hot in here. The room is a prayer oven. I can tell that the old lady who is the boss of the rosary has been doing it for a long time. She's really fast. The kneeling people can barely understand her fast words. Sometimes, they don't even realize they're supposed to do the response part. I find a perfect chair, jammed in a corner next to a big bureau. At first, I don't know any of the prayers, but then I join in on the part where they pray the Litany to the Holy Virgin. I even get on my knees to pray like everyone else. It's an easy prayer, everybody just says "pray for her" after each part, so I join in like a pro.

Holy Virgin of Virgins.
Pray for her.
Mother of Christ.
Pray for her.
Mother Undefiled.
Pray for her.
Queen of the Patriarchs.
Pray for her.

Mirror of Justice.
Pray for her.
Seat of Wisdom.
Pray for her.
Tower of Ivory.
Pray for her.
House of Gold.
Pray for her.
Mystical Rose.
Pray for her.

When I hear that, I stop praying. "Mystical Rose." That is the most beautiful thing I never heard, and I'm tripping out about how busy the Holy Mother must be if she has all those jobs, not just simple jobs like being mother of all the Mexicans and Catholics but also weird jobs like "Seat of Wisdom." Then I sit and listen. Kneeling in the corner in the dark, I feel invisible. That makes me happy. Nobody is looking at me. Nobody is saying anything about me. I like it in this room, with the women and the old guys and the Mystical Rose.

By the time we finish, everyone is hot and tired of kneeling. Ma tells me to help some of the older people get up. Ma thanks the señora who ran the rosary. I follow her, and when we get back outside, her best friend from high school, Pati the Mouth, comes up to hug her. I've heard since forever that Pati the Mouth was the biggest talker ever, and I can see that it's the truth. She sits Ma down on the sofa, gets right next to her, and immediately starts talking. The words and the spit waterfall out of her mouth.

"Hmmph. It was so unexpected," Pati says, "the way poor Doña Ofelia died. Dr. Maclobio saw her just last month, and he said she was overweight but healthy and that she would dance the dance of the hot huarache all over our graves and would you believe what the doctor did for his mother, which is so beautiful, he sent her on a trip to Roma and she got to see the first Easter Mass of his holiness Pope John Paul the Sixth, may God keep him, and, as if that wasn't enough, she also got to go to the Holy Land, and she walked the twelve stations of the cross like our Señor did, but she's always been a good walker, not like me, but I tried, you know, Chavela and I started walking, but you can't do anything in this neighborhood without everyone trying to copy you, and pretty soon we had five or six viejas joining us every day for a walk. Hmmph. They even brought the same walking shoes as us. The only thing left was for the dogs to be wearing those same sneakers."

She stops and wipes the corners of her mouth. "Hmmph, and speaking of dogs, you should have seen Don Antonio cry when his little mutt, Firulais, died. He did not weep for his own wife half the tears he wept for that dog. I don't see what he was so upset about, poor creature had cataracts and terrible gas, she must have been rotting from the inside out, I'd guess, and I tried to warn him, 'Don Antonio,' I'd say, 'are you feeding this dog dead rats or what?' Hmmph. Always some kind of tragedy in the neighborhood, no? Did you hear about El Cerebro. You remember Rosita's baby, with the really big head? Can't remember his real name, but everyone called the baby El Cerebro or sometimes El Charlie Brown, poor thing.

She had warned her old man about fixing the water boiler a thousand times, because it was making suspicious noises and shaking like Tongolele every time she got a cup of hot water, and of course, Mister No-Good Drunk didn't fix it, and one day that rusty old boiler exploded and the poor baby thing got scalded on his big Martian head."

I can tell Ma wants to add a word or two, but there's no room for it. Pati describes El Cerebro's burns, and Ma just shrinks into the sofa. I try to get Ma's attention, and when she finally looks at me, I give her the "I wanna go home" look, but she just gives me the "there's nothing I can do" look.

I go back into the living room and sit down to watch TV. It's *Happy Days*, but it's not. It's in Spanish, and the voices are all weird. Mr. C. sounds really young, and the Fonz, to tell the truth, sounds like a nerd. It's so warm that I doze off and don't wake up till Ma shakes me. I think Pati talked at her really hard, because Ma looks like she just got off of a roller coaster.

"Are you ready to leave?" she asks me.

"Yes, Ma. I'm ready to go." We walk back with the empty pozole pot. It is getting dark, so it is not so hot anymore. As we walk, I talk a little with Ma.

"Your friend Pati really likes to talk, doesn't she?"

"Yes," says Ma. "But remember that Pati is an adult, and you shouldn't be making fun of her, even if she talks too much."

"Okay, Ma," I say. "You sound really tired."

"I am. We drove all night, and now this wake, and tomorrow is the burial. We should get to bed early today."

The next morning, everyone is busy getting dressed for the burial. I take out my number two favorite shirt and put it on. Oh no. I haven't worn the shirt since Christmas, and now it fits really tight around my belly and my chest. The buttons look like they're trying to escape. I try to hold my belly in, but it doesn't help much, and besides, I can't hold it in all day. The only thing to do is wear a sweater vest, to cover up my poppin' fresh shirt. This really sucks, because it's going to be hot.

We drive to Doña Ofelia's house. When we arrive, a bunch of cars are there already. They are waiting for the funeral car. When it comes, I'm surprised. It's Roberto the Sasquatch in a white flatbed Ford pickup. The two brothers, three sisters, and one of Roberto's big boys help carry the coffin and put it into the back of the truck. Dang, I didn't even know girls could carry a coffin. Roberto and Clemencia, the biggest of the sisters, put ropes through the coffin handles and tie it to the hooks on the truck bed. Then they put the flowers in. The big, red heads of the roses are hanging down like sleepy wino heads. The gladiolus aren't looking very glad. The chrysanthemums are the worst of all. When Roberto loads them on the truck, they drop all kinds of petals. I was wrong to think the oleanders were crappy flowers, because they look fresher in their mayonnaise jar than any of the big arrangements.

The Sasquatch brothers climb into the white truck. The sisters get into cars with their husbands and kids. We all begin the trip to the cemetery. In our station wagon, we got the spot right behind the white truck, and we follow close behind so we won't get lost. We drive for a few minutes, then I notice that we've passed the Cachanilla Stadium twice.

"Pa, are we lost?"

"No."

"Well if we're not lost, why did we pass the stadium two times?"

"Because Ofelia loved going to the stadium for wrestling matches," says Pa. "And she always said that when she died, we should take her around three times."

My sister and I look at each other real quick, and I look the other way, because I can tell we are about to have a laughing attack, and since it's a funeral, Pa will for sure slap us across the head.

After the third lap, we continue down Avenida Juárez and then the white truck pulls over and everyone else does too.

"Pa, this isn't a graveyard," says Sylvie. "Why are we stopping here?"

"Remember Chon?"

"No."

"He was Ofelia's youngest son. Do you remember the redhead?"

"I think you two were still little kids when you last saw Chon," says Ma. "You probably don't remember him. He would take marijuana across into Calexico, and that is why he is in jail now."

"Chon lives in that big, gray building right there," says Pa. "It's a jail."

"They're taking Ofelia's coffin to jail?" I ask.

"No, that's not how they do this," says Pa. Roberto and his family untie the coffin and walk it up the stairs to the main door of the building. They open it up and walk back to their cars.

Two guards in dark green khaki shirts and pants bring Chon out. He is wearing a baggy prison suit the same gray color as the building. His hands are cuffed, and he is taking short steps because his legs are chained together. I can't see his eyes because of his sunglasses. His reddish hair is cut super short. His droopy red mustache looks like a big, sad mouth. He sees his family and waves at them. They wave back. Chon's eyebrows go up in the middle, and he looks sad. The guards open up the coffin for him. He looks down at her. It's like he looked at Medusa, because his face becomes stone. The lines on his forehead. His jaw. It's all stone. With the back of one hand, he touches her face very gently, like he's afraid to wake her up. The guards are really nice. They stand there and don't say nothing. Finally, he finishes looking and walks back with the guards into the building. His jail pants are all saggy in the back. His chains drag on the floor. He walks up the steps and he doesn't look back.

Before he goes into the entrance of the jail, the last guard signals to the family that they can come for the coffin. The brothers and sisters load the coffin back in the truck and tie it down again. The caravan of cars drives out of Mexicali, and pretty soon, all I see is dusty countryside: a few houses, bushes, and cactus. We arrive at El Centinela, the cemetery, in about thirty minutes. They let the truck with the coffin into the gates, and they ask everyone else to park outside. We get out of the car and begin walking through the cemetery. I look around at the graveyard. At first, most of the graves have little wooden crosses painted white with plastic roses and daisies, but when we get to the good neighborhood of the cemetery, the graves have big crosses made of cement or rock, with their names in it. Some have nice white statues of angels, Jesus Christ, or the Virgin of Guadalupe. We pass the grave of a lady who was named Aurelia Pacheco. Her gravestone has a little window in it, with her picture under the glass. It's a nice gravestone, except that inside her window, the glass had lots of drops of water, like tiny, tiny tears.

People are already circled around Doña Ofelia's spot. It still feels so normal, the way people are talking to each other while we wait. Tomorrow, everyone will keep doing what they always do, except they won't see Doña Ofelia, and it probably won't make a big difference anyway.

The priest arrives. He welcomes everyone and says he is Father Max Santamaria. The top of Father Santamaria's head is pink and sweaty. He drinks from his water bottle and begins. "This is a sad day, for we must say farewell to our beloved sister, Ofelia Rojas. Ofelia loved wrestling matches, mariachi music, swimming in the ocean at San Felipe, and cooking family dinners. She was the mother of three sons, Roberto, Tavo, and Chon. She was the mother of three loving daughters, Anita, Teresita, and Clemencia. Ofelia had fourteen grandchildren and two great-grandchildren, and she loved them all. For Ofelia, family was everything, and we should now be happy that she has rejoined her own mother, Elpidia, and her father, Salvador, and her sister Jesusita at the side of God in a place without pain, without sadness. The only sad ones are the people assembled here, who will miss her so much. Please join me in a moment of silence before the mariachis play the music she loved best."

Mariachi is the music of Pa drinking with his friends all night and playing the songs again and again, so usually I hate it, but today everything is different. The trumpet player lifts the trumpet to his mouth, and it cries. I feel the beginning of "Volver, Volver" cutting through my chest, and I finally understand why the drunk guys scream like women when this song comes on. It feels like you'll never stop being sad, never stop wishing you weren't a loser, but you are. You lose things. You lose people and you can't get them back. It almost feels good to listen to the song and admit the sad truth, and start bawling like a baby, which is what everyone's doing now. The Sasquatches finally get it. Tavo covers his face with his chubby fingers. Roberto's crying face is twisted up like he's laughing, but he's not. He's really sad, and he stares at the coffin. Anita and Teresita, the Sasquatch sisters, hug each other and cry. Clemencia, the oldest of them all, is the toughest. Her face shows nothing, but the tears keep coming down her cheeks.

The mariachi sing the part about how much you want to go back, back, back to the one you loved. But you can't. It's too late to go back. It's too late for anything but a sad song and a quick goodbye.

I look up at my mami. She has her eyes closed and still the tears sneak out. Even though I hardly know Doña Ofelia, I start crying too. I move a little bit, so the sleeve of my shirt touches my mami's arm. While I stand there with my sleeve touching her, the trumpets cry out the last bit of the song, and a breeze carries it into the desert.

Acknowledgments

M any people have directly and indirectly helped make *Gordo* possible. I thank my family elders, who were the first great storytellers in my life. I thank James Weir, my first creative writing teacher at Watsonville High School. I thank my pre-gentrification San Francisco village of artists, activists, intellectuals, and *mal vivants*, who were the first community to see me and invite every bit of me to the party (Pato Hebert, Tisa Bryant, Jorge Cortiñas, Wura Ogunji, Vero Majano, Horacio Roque, Adela Vasquez, Ricardo Bracho, Sarah Patterson, Lito Sandoval, Diane Felix, Joel Tan, and Al Lujan, among others). You were the first community I wanted to make art for and with. I thank Dorothy Allison, Reinaldo Arenas, David Wojnarowicz, Toni Cade Bambara, Jean Genet, Richard Rodriguez, Hermann Hesse, and David Sedaris for lighting my way.

I thank my editor, John Freeman, and my agent, Frances Coady, for their expert guidance and support. I especially thank Rebecca Solnit for modeling writerly excellence, believing in these stories, and championing them with such determination and generosity.